To ████, from
one traveler to another

Enjoy

Capt. ████████

MEMORIES OF A BOATMAN

Bob Covey

authorHOUSE®

AuthorHouse™
1663 Liberty Drive
Bloomington, IN 47403
www.authorhouse.com
Phone: 1-800-839-8640

First published by AuthorHouse   3/18/2010

ISBN: 978-1-4490-9097-5 (e)
ISBN: 978-1-4490-9096-8 (sc)

Library of Congress Control Number: 2010902265

Printed in the United States of America
Bloomington, Indiana

This book is printed on acid-free paper.

Chapter 1

I got a phone call and am asked to come aboard the whaler as a crewmember. This is good news for me so off to the whaling I go.

Got on board and stowed my gear and then went to the wheelhouse. There are three men in there. One is my brother and the other two I had seen around before. Bud is the skipper and Bill, Dave and I are the crew.

Bud's first question is, "have you done any whaling before?"

"No I haven't but maybe I can learn."

"Well you had better or off you go."

He told us to get the vessel ready for sea.

We got busy and about 10 hours later we were ready. Hell of a lot to it besides "Let's go."

" Stay away from the harpoons and the ammo. Until you are shown what it is all about."

"Ok, let's go and get a whale."

In the navy I had served aboard a vessel just like this one. I knew my way around. This was a minesweeper and has been converted to whaling. The forward gun and the railings have been removed so that the harpoon can be turned without running into them. Also she has been double planked.

We all had many things to do. The navy had about 70 men on these boats and we are only 4.

One day I cook another maybe running the engines or steering or navigating.

At night we tried to be close to the Farallon Islands so that we could tie up to the buoy and not have to drop the anchor. If we have to anchor it is necessary to keep a watch in case the anchor drags on the bottom. One morning there were 6 boats tied up to us. The first guy up blew the whistle and those boats cast off and left.

We got underway and then I cooked breakfast. We always are looking for whales but we try to eat every chance that we get. More than once it was necessary to throw everything into the sink and get after a whale.

We got after this whale and it is now 2hours since we started the chase. It has not been able to blow much and is getting tired and the last time it came up was about 15 minutes ago and now we are very close. Now we can see the swirls in the water and the whale birds are very exited so get ready. Bill is on the gun and alert. Here it comes and the distance is perfect and the shot is true. Now we have a whale.

By the time that the line becomes tight, Dave is on the winch and starts to pay out and heaves up as needed. It has been an instant kill so I get the gear ready to tie up the whale alongside. We have the whale alongside and almost through with the tie up when the skipper hollers 'Thar she blows, 2 points off the starboard and less than a half mile."

Had to make sure that the whale was full of air. I have a pipe that is attached to the compressor and I put that into the whale about 4 feet and the compressor takes only about 5 minutes to pump it full. The whale has to float while we chase the next one.

The skipper checks our present position so that we can get back to this whale.

Here we go. Bill has the harpoon gun loaded and ready. Dave secures the winch and gets the 3 inch line attached to the harpoon and the winch line. By this time we are at top speed and I am on the engines and steering. Dave comes up and takes over the steering.

We can see the whale now and it has spotted us. It takes only about 5 blows and sounds. We know that it will not be able to stay down long. The whale birds are all exited and we are ready. Here she comes and we are right there. Another good shot and now we have two whales.

The whale is alongside and now we have to rig it for towing. This one is on the starboard side and the rigging is attached. I have it pumped up with air even though we are not going after another because it will tow better. We got the other one after an hours search. I was surprised at how far it had floated. Dave told me that next time we will attach a high buoy so we can see it better.

Now is the long tow into the whaling plant that is near Point Richmond. The weather is good with plenty of visibility, light wind and no traffic. It looks as though we will get to the sea buoy on the last of the ebb tide. It is not possible to make much speed although the engines are working hard.

Now is the time to get some chow. Dave, Bill and I drew high card to see who would cook. Dave drew a six, Bill got a ten so I knew that I had a good chance. Not so I got a four. Hell I didn't want to cook anyhow.

It took about four hours to get to the sea buoy and another hour to get to mile rock. By that time the tide was starting to flood so we picked up speed and got abeam Angel Island and around into the Richmond Channel. Bud had called in and told the plant that we were coming with a double so they were ready for us.

Check the fuel, water etc. and make sure that we have enough food. Dave, check the harpoons, ammo etc. As soon as we can, I want to get underway and get more whales.

These were orders from the skipper so guess I now am part of the crew for sure.

Those two whales measured 61 feet for one and the other is 52. Going to get a good payday. We get paid per foot and nothing if there are no whales.

The weather report is favorable and here we go. If the wind picks up it is impossible to spot a blow and our chances are reduced to zero.

The sea buoy is on our port side and look at that. Right ahead at about I mile is the nicest blow that the skipper has seen in a long time. He said "Men that is a blue and let's not miss him."

How he knew that it is a blue I don't know but it turned out to be one.

We went into battle stations and everyone was ready. Bill made sure that a spear was all set up in case it was needed. It would be used in the event that the first shot did not kill the whale. The spear was set with a warhead and had to be handled with care.

Bud maneuvered the boat right into position and Bill fired the harpoon and made a good shot. It looked as though the spear would be needed so into the gun it went and was fired and also was a good shot. The whale is dead and now we have to get it alongside. Got it all rigged and made ready for the tow. This whale is huge and makes for a tough job to steer and make any headway. Took us four hours to get back under the bridge but the flood was running so now the tide made it easier. Bud called the plant and they thought that he is kidding. He said, " Those guys had better wake up because this one is a big one."

Guess the plant is not finished with the other whales that we had brought in. They all came out on the dock to see. After we got the whale secured alongside the float we stayed tied up. Bud said that he wants to see this. We got some chow and checked things over and made sure that we could get underway if needed.

About 3 hours later the crew from the plant came out and looked things over. They rigged the lines onto the whale and watered down the slip and got ready to pull it up. They heaved it up until the lines were taut and stopped. They then rigged up some more lines and then put more strain onto them and the whale did start up the slip. All of a sudden the blocks tore loose and one of them went out the side of the building and into the street.

We had measured the length of the whale. It is 80feet long and will be another good payday.

Whales weigh right on to one ton per foot so this one is 80 tons.

The weather report is still good so Bud told the plant to keep the spear and the harpoon and we will pick them up next trip. We got underway and headed back to sea.

The sea buoy is astern us about 2 miles and Dave said, "Look at that mess ahead."

He had seen the whitecaps and they got worse as we watched.

Bud gave orders to head for the island and we will stay there for a day or so and maybe this will flatten out. Two days later we got underway and started back in and about an hour later I hollered "Thar she blows. Astern of us about ¼ mile." Bud told me to quit fooling around.

"Well, dam I had the impression that this is a whaler but guess not."

That made Bud look back at me and in doing so he saw another blow. " Thar, oh shit someone already said that."

We came about and headed for battle stations.

All of a sudden Bud slowed down and got on the mike and told us to forget it because as of this morning these Humpback Whales are declared endangered and off the list.

This was just the beginning of those environmentalists and their insidious ways.

One of the whaleboats tied up a whale to the buoy off Ocean Beach and someone reported it as a capsized boat. The Coast Guard did not like that and the skipper of that boat almost lost his license. He had thought that he could leave it there while he went for another whale.

We turned and started in and Bill thought he saw a blow off our port side and we all watch for it. Yep, there is a blow so here we go again. This one turned out to be a sperm whale so we went on the hunt. Sperm whales have teeth and they are very valuable. They also are able to stay down for 45 minutes or more. It is a real challenge to get one.

" Count the number of blows and one of you guys go get some coffee. This is going to take awhile."

It is now about 2 hours since we first saw the blow and we still don't have the whale. It will be dark in another 4 hours. We saw this one when he breached and he is a big one. Bud thinks that he has been hunted before. The birds are getting excited and sure enough here he comes and this time we are right on him. He only got 2 blows so he won't be able to stay down long and we will get a shot soon. Here he comes. Bill is ready and as soon as that whale got up he put a shot into him. It is a good shot and that whale is dead. We got it all rigged and ready for towing and headed in to the plant.

This whale will have a lot of sperm oil, which is worth a lot. Dave usually extracts the oil at the plant. He has tried to get someone else trained but so far he has to be on top of it. This one looks to be about 65 feet long so between the length, teeth and oil we should have another good payday.

The Fish and Game people were given a list of whales that may now be harvested. This list is given to all the whalers and now we have to be real careful. One of the boats brought in a restricted one and they had to pay a $1500 fine.

Supposed to be good weather so back to sea we go.

Thar she blows. Two points on the starboard bow about 2 miles. Here we go again. There are several blows and Bud thinks that they are Grays. He looked at the list and we are allowed 25/yr. He said, "That is 25 for the whole fleet and not just this boat." He got on the radio and could not find out of any that have been taken so far.

I looked up to the north and saw whitecaps. "We had better work fast because whitecaps and wind are coming."

We made a kill and got one Gray ready to tow in time before the wind hit us. Nothing to do now but go in to the plant.

These Grays are not very big and this one is only about 35 feet long.

The plant had been able to get that big Blue cut up and into the works so our spot was clear.

The weather report got worse and we had to stay at the dock.

We went over to the fuel dock and took on a full load and checked over the boat. Had to take on some stores but with all this BS about the limiting the catch we wondered just how much. We are now allowed per year 5 Fins, no more Blues, no Humpbacks and the Grays are limited. Looks like this is going to be the deathblow for Whaling.

Chapter 2

It was a tough deal getting into the Union let alone getting a job. Not only just registering as seeking a job but it was necessary to pay money. Not after you got a job but up front and right now. Made it real tough on anyone that was short. Some guys borrowed from one of the other members and then they were charged high interest and had a dead line as to when the loan had to be paid off. That caused a lot of trouble and sometimes it got real nasty. The Union did not guarantee that you would get a job and I know men that waited for weeks to finally get a dispatch.

Each day Mon. thru Fri. at ten in the morning the men would gather in the Hall and wait for the calls for any jobs available. Some days there were several jobs on the board and then the guy with the most seniority would show his card to the boss and the boss would check to see whether the man had all the dues and assessments paid up. If those were current the man would be considered OK for the job. In the case where there was only one job on the board the same procedure was followed. Sometimes the man with the most seniority did not want the job it was then given to the next one. Of course the same procedure of dues etc. was followed.

There was a time when men could be hired off the dock according to his knowledge and willingness to work. The union seemed to put money first and seniority next.

When the whalers came into the Hall looking for work we were accepted right in. It seemed that most of the men looking for work had no sea time and had only worked on day boats there in the harbor. I got a dispatch that lasted 3 years. I had sea time and was not afraid of work. The other whalers got good jobs and did not have to spend time cooling their heels in the Hall. At that time the initiation fee was $500 and the dues were $20 per month. Hard to come by for some of the men.

My dispatch told me to report the next morning to the tug Sea Lion that was tied up at Pier 3 in S.F. After signing in and stowing my gear, all hands were told to get on deck and prepare for getting underway. We backed out from the dock and headed for Redwood City, which was a short run from pier 3.

I did not know any of the men on the crew and as time went on and was dispatched to other boats and other runs I was to get used to new men to ship with. A full crew for sea duty consisted of Skipper, first mate, second mate, engineer, 2 ab"s and 1 deckhand and 1 cook. There were times that the cook seemed to be the most important member.

The Captain turned out to be an <old salt> and was a good man as well as a good teacher. He and I got along well and he started teaching me and the education was very thorough. Sometimes it was very hard to learn all the things that he was teaching but he was patient and did not seem to be put out of shape if he had to repeat the lesson or lessons. Thanks to him I was able to advance up the ladder and got a better job with more pay. He was called 'snowball' and since he did not have white hair I was curious as to the story about that nickname. I asked him a couple times but he would not tell me the story until about 2 months later.

We were up in the wheelhouse and the weather was fine and we were sort of taking it easy. All of a sudden he said ' Guess it is about time to tell you the story of my nickname'.

'About 8 or nine years ago we were tied up over in Guam and we had to wait for a barge to be loaded and made ready for sea. The estimated time to finish the barge was 1 week. I had been wanting to get the mast and the rest of the rigging painted but this was the first time that we were at the dock and in calm water. The rigging and mast was all black painted and would take a lot of time to chip and scrape and then do the painting. Everyone of the deck crew took turns and finally got the prep work done. The deckhand was sent up to do some of the painting and was told over and over to be careful with the paint. Guess he thought he had it all under control and became careless. Just as I was walking up to look at the job the bucket of black paint upset and cascaded down onto my head. Never did figure out what really happened and gave him the benefit of doubt and called it an accident. Be as it may I have had that nickname of 'snowball' ever since.' From then on any time that I have to look at some painting being done in the rigging I always go down to the main deck and use my binoculars. He was the best and nicest Capt that I ever had.

Chapter 3

Next trip out I went as 2nd mate. He was still the Capt and he never did let up on the teaching. There were times that it was so busy that I got only a few hours sleep at a time but I was young and could take the long hours.

We got the boat ready and after going through the checkoff list we fired up and headed for Redwood City. We were to pick up a tow for Alaska. This tow was a converted ship that was used only for hauling cement. It was rigged with a bridle and was supposed to be all ready to go. Snowball taught me that just because someone says that it is in fine shape, check it over really well anyhow. Sure enough I found a crack in one of the links in the bridle. We called in a repair man from our shipyard and he had it fixed up in a few hours. If that had broken out at sea we could have been in real trouble.

It did not take very long to get the tow rigged and we had put out one shot of chain as the weather is never just O. K. and out there it would have been impossible to make changes. A shot of chain is 90 ft.

long and acts as shock cord as it's heavy weight holds the tow line down and keeps the line from fetching up and possibly becoming so tight that the line can part. If we anticipate really heavy weather we can add another shot of chain but generally one shot will do the job.

We got away from the dock and out in the stream and started towards the Bay Bridge. I called the vessel traffic center and reported our intentions and our destination. Their reply was thank you and good sailing. If there had been traffic in the Bay the traffic center would have told me what and where so that I would be able to take the proper cautions and set a good course. There are times that the Bay has a lot of ships and boat traffic and getting that ship and tug along in good shape was a challenge. At last we made it to the Golden Gate and it was a relief to feel the lift of the sea and it was now O.K. to add rpms and pick up speed. Here we go and as soon as we could we started to pay out tow line. Out at sea we usually had around 1800 ft. of tow line out and made sure that it streamed well. The weather was fair and so I got a relief and had a cup of coffee.

Just aft of the tow winch I tied a piece of small line to the tow line and if for some reason the tow winch brake slipped it would be easy to tell as the line would go out with the tow line. Looking aft at night it might be impossible to see the tow back there but that line tied on would be seen easily. One of the questions I would ask was where is the small line? It did not take many lessons to have that line checked very often. Sometimes the person that was my fellow watch stander would just get settled in his chair and was having coffee I would ask the line question. Soon they would give me a report on the line without my asking anymore.

We ran on a west course until we cleared the sea buoy and then headed north. It was a good idea to stay out away from the traffic that was always in near shore. I knew a guy that thought it was funny to go in fairly close so that he could run the barges over crab pots etc. I told him what a lousy thing to do but I might as well talk to the bulkhead as he would not change. I would not ship with him.

This trip turned out to be really nice as far as the weather goes. The ship that we were towing was easy and stayed in line well. There have been tows that I have had that would shear off from side to side and cause the boat to shudder as though it would come apart. In that case it was hard to maintain a course and we would end up with a wheel wash looking like a snake had come along. We got out away from most of the fishing boats and then changed course to NW and headed for Alaska.

The cook came up to the wheelhouse and asked what I wanted for supper and I said that he had better ask Snowball. He said he had talked to him and his reply was ' ask the mate". The cook was a man that I had known for a long time and so I thought that it would be a good idea if he would just do the cooking. I believe that he could cook just about anything and it would taste fine. He was the best cook on the west coast as far as I was concerned.

If the weather had gotten rough and the boat was bouncing up and down I would have asked for some "lumpys". That was the name for hotcakes if it was merely rough but if it were rough and cold I would ask for chest protectors. Most of the cooks had a real hard time making hotcakes that were not all over the pan during the heaving and yawing of the boat in heavy weather. Johnny's were round and you would think that we were tied up at the dock. In my estimation he was a master chef.

The weather remained calm with a small lump and we could keep the engine at full throttle and even had time to enjoy the scenery and watch the sea creatures. Whales, sea lions, and lots of birds. Sometimes it looked as though there was a great river ahead with a rapids and white water. It would turn out to be hundreds of porpoise, jumping and sometimes coming clear out of the water. They would put on a show for us and I think that they enjoyed the chance to show off.

When we were running at full throttle the engine was turning over at about 940 rpms. And we could make 10 knots and we would cover a lot of distance and Keni Peninsula was getting closer every 24 hours. In fact it seemed as though the trip would be over too quick. We had plenty of stores aboard and the best cook on the west coast.

Capt. Snowball made sure that we maintained a good distance off the coast. Along Oregon the coast can be really hazardous as there are rocks way out away from the shoreline. If we were running at night or any other time that we were using radar as a navigational aid it would be real important to know our position. Radar does not pick up low targets in many cases. A mountain might be 20 miles inland and the radar can pick it up on the screen but the low beaches and rocks might not show and so-stay out and give that coast lots of sea room. We always made sure that we had good up to date charts and paid attention to them. The tow line was out there 1800 to 2000 ft. and if for some reason there was slack in the line it would sink down and would be in danger if there were rocks or bottom too close. I know of one boat that did not pay attention and as a result it was dragged down and sank and all hands were lost.

Our trip on up to the cement dock went along real well and the weather actually was good and not much wind and not much fog. We thought that we would have time off while the cement was being unloaded. A radio transmission came through and told us to help steady a drilling rig out in the Keni. So here w go. Got out there and the tide was running about 14 knots and that rig was having a tough time holding position. We got a line on it and steadied it and after 2 days they were able to get their anchors set and were in a solid footing. A call came in that the ship was unloaded and ready to leave so back to the dock and we got the bridle and tow line rigged and away we went. No rest for a tugboatman.

The empty ship handled well even though it was way up there and usually a high target like that made the wind real happy and would buffet the tow so that we would have considerable problems with maintaining a course. This ship settled down and we could make a good speed.

We got into SF and up to Redwood City and had the boat tied up and all headed for Pier 3 and a nice payoff. As soon as we were paid off we headed for our homes. Some guys lived a long ways from SF and they usually went back to the hall to check on the possibility that there might be another boat that needed a crew. I was only 2hrs. from home so off I went to see the family. That trip up and back to Alaska only took about 1 month and as it turned out it was one of the fastest trips that I will make in years.

Chapter 4

Sure was nice to be home and of course I thought that I would have some time to kick back and enjoy the family but it does not work that way for a sea going tug man. Three days later I got a call from the tug office and they told me to report at 0700 to the tug Sea Lion. The company supplied the parking so at 0430 I headed for SF and parked on pier 3 and left a company tidebook on the dashboard. The tidebook was used to identify that I was an employee and to leave the vehicle alone.

No one was aboard when I got there so I made myself at home and put on a pot of coffee. One by one men showed and I did not know any of them until the engineer came. He was the same one that was on that Alaska trip.

One of the guys made the remark that he was to ship as second mate. Well guess I must have been put back as a deckhand. The Capt came on board and it was Snowball again. I wanted the lower bunk starboard side in the forecastle so I got my gear and started down the ladder. I had only gotten down the first step when I heard Snowball holler and he said " where the hell are you going- your bunk is topside". Wow I was 1st mate.

While I was home the boat had been fueled, the fresh water tank filled, the oil reserve tank had been filled and stores had been loaded. It seemed that all the work had been done. I was soon to find out that everything had to be checked over and that a list had to be made and each item marked down. All the charts that we were to need for this next trip had to be laid out and ready and put in the order that they would be needed. Good job for the second mate. All the lines etc. had to be checked, and a hundred other things had to be done. Snowball taught me to check everything while we were at the dock and make sure all's well. Even after the checks it seemed that something was missed but we did the best that we could.

Our orders were to pick up a derrick barge in Willapa Bay and take it to Anacortes. We cast off the lines and got underway and headed out the

Golden Gate. The ocean was flat calm and the wind was only light airs so we hooked it on and got a bone in her teeth as soon as we had cleared the Gate. We made a fast trip and it seemed that we were off the Columbia in record time. Willapa Bay is not very far north of the Columbia. It is easy to get into the bay and until we had gotten into the bay we had lots of room but as we got close to the town the channel narrowed down. It was high tide so we could look into the stores as we went by. It looked as though the whole town had come out to see the boat going by. Afterward I always wondered how much money had changed hands with the betting as to whether we would make it or not. The boat was 121 feet long and the place where we had to turn around allowed us about 20 feet to work in. Snowball had a way with boats and sure put her around without too much trouble.

The barge was tied up with the bow down stream so we put our stern right up to her and made up a tow. The barge had a good bridle and we made up to that directly with the tow line. I think that half of the people in the town had followed us and so there were plenty of hands to throw off the dock lines so that saved us a little time. We wanted to take advantage of the high water and get on down to the main bay. After we got down to deep water we put out 1 shot off chain and went aboard to check the deck and the lights on the barge. We had to sign a paper that said that we were not to go over 6 knots. The barge had a large crane and since the barge was narrow beam it had to be treated carefully.

We got all the things taken care of and we were ready to head out to sea. Instead of just leaving and since the cook had dinner ready we ate first. It was nice to be able to set a cup down without it taking off across the table.

Well here we go and the weather report was that we should have good going.

There was only about 20ft of water going out of the bay into the ocean so we had to keep the chain aboard and the tow line short until we got out to deep water. We went on the slow bell and made it out to the sea buoy and out to the 10 fathom mark and then we let the chain go. Next we started to stream out wire and headed for 30 fathoms where we turned to a course that would put us close to the Straits. We stayed on about 345degrees and shot for Destruction Island which is just south of the Straits. It took us about 3 days to get there because we had to keep the speed down to 6knots. The weather held and we entered the Straits in good shape

It was night time and one of those black nights that makes it hard to distinguish shapes, boats or anything else. I turned on the radar and kept a close watch. Even the radar can not see into the water and all of a sudden there was a bump at the bow. The noise continued the length of the boat and I figured that maybe we had gotten into serious trouble. It turned out though that the main trouble was just the noise. We did not have to come to a stop, anyhow in order to stop it would have taken a mile or so. The bump was a large log and they are always a hazard.

We got abeam of Port Angeles and it was just getting light. We wanted to get to Anacortes in the daylight so we were in good shape. It was slack water and not much of a current so heaved up the wire and put the chain on deck and came alongside the barge and made up for a starboard landing and tie up at the dock. The new crew was working out fine so there was not much time involved in the change. Put up a spring line, bow line, and a stern line and the barge was not a big one so we had good control. I called the dock and told them to use their lines for tie up if necessary and they said " no problem".

We got tied up and all secure and I figured that we would have a little time off, at least an hour or so. Guess what? No such luck. The port captain came down to the boat and told me that we were to take that barge that we could see ahead of us to Arness Terminal in the Kenii south of Anchorage.

First things first. The second mate and I went to the wheelhouse and checked to make sure that the right charts were on board. They were and all the inside passage charts were complete. So now we had to make up a tow and get going. We were told that when we got up there we had to run anchors for the drilling rig until relieved.

We got the tow rigged and had to do some ordering of some other stores so by that time it was about 2200 hrs. The stores were delivered about 0430 and by the time it got light we were ready to leave. I called vessel traffic center and they advised us to wait. There was some big ship traffic and since we had to leave the dock and turn they felt as though it would be safer to wait and they would advise us. Good time for some chow. The cook was up and in the galley. He made a nice breakfast and we had time to actually sit down and eat without being in a hurry. About an hour later traffic center called and gave us the OK. "all hands on deck-prepare to get underway".

The crew knew their jobs and at my order they cast off the bow line, stern line and the spring line. The man on the dock jumped back onto the barge and then got ready to cast off the lines to the boat. We moved away from the dock and got out into the stream and then let go the barge lines and took her in tow. After the lines were all secured and stowed for sea we went to sea watches. Each man stood 4hr watches.

Chapter 5

We went up Puget Sound and across the Straits and on up to Strait of Georgia leaving Victoria on our starboard side. Just before Seymour it was necessary to shorten up the tow line as it is tough going through the narrows.

Seymour Narrows is as it says "narrows". We can make it through but be careful. The tides run real fast both on the flood or on the ebb.

Arrived at Queen Charlotte Sound around 2000hrs. Got to Prince Rupert at around 2000hrs twenty-four hours later. It is a trip that all people should take if possible. We saw thousands of birds and it would have been nice if I had the time to get out a book and see whether or not I could identify each of them. Coming around guard rock was slow going and the water was not that deep and the wheel wash caused the salmon to be brought up and the eagles had a field day. The bird protectors say that there is a shortage of them and have them on the list. If that is the case and they are in short numbers, where did those hundreds come from?

Instead of staying in the Queen Charlottes we kept in close to the eastern side and then went into Fitz Hugh Sound and on to Milbank Sound by way of Bella Bella. It was nice to at last reach Greenville

Channel as it was a lot wider and almost straight. From there it was an easy run up to Ketchikan. It was a real town and had real buildings etc. Some of the cruise ships stop there and the passengers get to look around and walk the streets. We of course had to keep right on going. We went on and back into Clarence Straits and on to Snow Pass.

Snow Pass is a tough spot to negotiate but after we got passed that we were in some good going. We went up Frederick Sound to Chatham Strait and over to Icy Strait. There were many small ice-bergs floating and it was necessary to use all lot of care. These were translucent and blue to turquoise and were a sight to see. Always enjoyed going through this area as it is sure pretty but it was necessary to use care.

When we got close to Cape Spencer I slowed down and heaved up wire so that we could go on the slow bell. The cook got some food ready and the crew had a chance to eat before we got out into the open ocean. The newest weather report was not favorable and also had to put up storm windows. I had learned the hard way to get those windows ahead of heavy weather. They were made of plywood and were affixed to the bulkhead and covered the forward windows. A 6 inch hole allowed a person to see out and ahead. There was one hole on the port side and one on the starboard side and it was real important to have the radar on and adjusted. Can't see much through a 6 inch hole.

Streamed out wire and got ready for sea and made it out past the light and turned for Cook's Inlet. It was a 600 mile run and for the first day and night it was rough going and had to run on the slow bell. The weather started to get better and a north wind blew only about 6 knots and laid the ocean down and it was a nice ride the rest of the way into the inlet. We made it to Arness Terminal and got tied up and left the barge there and headed for the rig tending business. The Foster Parker rig had to be held in place against the tide and we did so without any trouble. A diver was to cut the holding bolts on the float with the idea that at the correct moment we were to give the float a sharp tug and break the remaining bolts. The tide had let up and it was slack water and we had let go of the rig and were getting ready to hook-up to the float when all of sudden the float broke loose. The rig sank on that side and went into a steep angle and dumped 10 workmen into the water. There was pack ice floating in the area so they only had a few minutes before they would die from exposure. Man overboard!! And this is no drill!

Sure glad that we had brought our tow line up on deck so we were able to maneuver and get in close. We were able to get 9 of the guys aboard real quick but that last guy could not even lift his arms and was trying to get his teeth onto the line that we had thrown. I had a life jacket on and we attached a line to me and in the drink I went. I did not have to go far to get to him and the crew pulled us in real fast. All of the men off the rig were sent by small boat into Soldatna where there is a hospital. They all had hypothermia but they were treated and back on the job in a week. I spent about 3hrs down in the engine room getting warm. Another day for a tugman.

The diver had cut too many bolts. Two bolts were to be left in place but guess he forgot to count. Foster Parker got one of their tugs to stand by and we were relieved to run anchors for the Conoco rig. We stayed on that job for 26 days and then were told to go to Anchorage and take on stores and fuel etc. We spent two days taking on fuel,fresh water and stores and were told to head for San Francisco. Since we were running light i.e. no tow we made a fast trip on down to the city. It took us a little over 7 days to make the trip. The crew was paid off and everyone went home for some R-R.

It would have been nice if I could have time off but 3 days after getting home a phone call came from Crowley and for me to report at 0700 two days later. Hard for a sea going tugman to get time off. Oh well the pay was good and the weather was nice so what am I griping about? This was a new boat and a whole new crew. It wasn't a new boat in the sense of "just built" but it was the first time that I had sailed in her. First thing was to take on stores, fuel, water, and check all the gear to see whether it was all on board. That turned out to be a big job as I had to order and wait for some of the stuff to be brought aboard. At last we were ready to head to sea. New orders came in and we had to go up to the Straits of Juan de Fuca and to Vancouver and take a barge up to Anchorage. Here we go again, up the inside passage.

I had a new mate and since the mates job was to make sure that all the charts are up to date and all complete. After about 3hours he came to me and said that all the charts were on board and accounted for. I said what about the charts for down the coast to SF. He said "I will have to check". Another 2hours and his report was they are all here except for a couple. " Give me a report as to them". I put them onto an order list to be delivered to Anchorage. It turned out that all the charts from Trading Bay to Purdue Bay were missing. That was put on the report so that they could be added and

picked up in SF.

The 2nd mate was a guy from Idaho. His wife stayed home and ran the RV park that they had just south of Twin Falls.

Many of the men had wives that took care of business at home. One had a hotel in SF, another a service station, grocery store and post-office. They were an interesting group of men. The 2nd mate had 10 years at sea and had used his money well. Of course there were guys that made their investments at the bars etc.

We finally got all the details taken care of and we were ready to get underway. One of the deck crew came to me and said that one of the men had to go do something in town and had not returned yet. "Ok I'll wait 30 minutes for him but if he is not here by then we'll go anyhow and you guys will have to stand extra duty to make up for his not being on board". 29 minutes later I gave the order to single up and be ready to cast off . It would be a hardship on all hands because of one guy missing. At the last second I looked up the dock with the hope that he would be coming. There he was all right running like he was a track star and waving his arms to get my attention. It happened to be high water so the boat was right up to the level of the dock and he never even slowed up and jumped on board. Behind him and down the dock a ways were some women running and I guess hollering. He let me know to throw off that last line and get going . So I did. We moved away from the dock and the women were jumping up and down and if the engines were not so loud I would have been able to learn some new language from them. WOW! That man reported to the wheelhouse as soon as the mate relieved him and told me a story.

It went something like this.

We have been right here for a couple days and doing things to get ready for sea and my clothes had gotten dirty so I wanted to change. It was then that I realized that for some reason my sea bag with all my gear was missing.

Before coming on board the other day we had a big celebration and going away party and one thing led into another and I ended up here on the boat. We went to work in the morning and I did not even think about the sea bag. It seemed that I would have plenty of time to go home and get the bag before we shoved off for sea. At home there were a bunch of women and they all thought that I should stay home and my wife got real nasty and I knew that my only chance was to get out of there, now. Again the sea bag was left and I am on the way to Alaska without any clothes except what I have on.

What a story. I have heard lots of them and it is not usually serious. Here is a guy that will really be up a creek without foul weather gear, let alone no change of anything. All the crew chipped in and got enough clothes to keep him going. When we got up to Anacortes we were able to get some more stuff for him.

Chapter 6

It seems that we had made such good time getting to Anacortes that we were to wait at least two days for the barge to be ready. Instead of just waiting and lying around I wanted things done.

"Joe you had better adjust the after winch"

"Bill, I want the fuel filters changed and make sure that there are enough extras so if necessary we can change them again 3 times. It takes 7 filters to make a change. Please count carefully."

Changing filters out at sea with a hot engine is no fun and can be real dangerous. The engine has to be shut down and if we have a tow it can catch up to us and sink the boat.

A few years before, we were running low on fuel so I decided to go into a fuel dock at Hoonah and top off. The man at the dock told me that he had lots of fuel and so I said fill-er up. It took 22,000 gals to top off. By the way, the boat used diesel for fuel. If all had gone well we could have gone all the way down to San Pedro and back to SF. But it was not to be.

Guess we must have almost emptied the tanks at the dock and in so doing all the muck and debris from the bottom had been transferred into the boat. We ran for about 24hours and all of a sudden the rpms went down and the engine was stopping so I had to stop it. The barge that we were to deliver to San Pedro did not and was coming at us. We only had a few minutes to get new filters in the fuel line. It was touch and go whether or not we could change the filters and then get the engine going in time. It was hot and the filters could not be handled with bare hands and that made one more hassle. The crew all worked together and we had about two lengths of the barge between us and a collision. Only that the barge is a whole lot bigger than the boat and will run right over us and sink us. The engine started right up and did not shut down so off we went. One more day in the life of a tugman.

Everything went well until we got between Duxbury Reef and the Farralones and the engine quit again. Another filter drill and I called in for a tug to stand by until we were able to make it into SF bay. We gave the barge over to the other tug and we went to the yard to get the tanks cleaned.

Two days later with all hands helping, the tanks were cleaned and refilled and we were ready to get the barge and continue on to San Pedro.

I learned a lot from that experience. Clean filters and never let a fuel dock use up all of their fuel to fill up my boat.

We got the barge all set up and looked over. It was necessary to make sure that while the barge had been sitting at the dock some one had not screwed up the gear etc. Everything looked OK so called vessel traffic center and they said that the way was clear and that no ship was near so away we went. Once again it was sure nice to be underway and headed out to sea. The reports from the weather station said that it would be light airs and flat ocean. Well 2hours later when we were rounding the sea buoy and set a course for San Pedro the wind had already picked up to 20 knots and looked like it was not going to slow down. Sure enough it got worse and soon was up to 25knots out of the north so we had a following sea and that made steering a little tough. We had put out one shot of chain and it seemed to do just fine.

We had a good run on down to the Santa Barbara and then the Santa Anna Wind started to blow and soon all was covered with sand. I had to start up the radar because the visibility was down to almost zero. Each time that I would lean over the radar tears would drop on the screen and my eyes were burning real bad. It must have blown like that for hours. At last we got down past the winds and was able to make it in to San Pedro without any more problems. We tied up at the Matson Shipping dock and were told to standby.

Each time that I got the orders to "standby" I started to think [now what]?

A container barge was being loaded with empty containers and sure enough we got orders to take it to SF. It towed real well and we had a good fast trip back to the city. The Santa Anna winds had quit and the north wind had died down 15 knots. We got a break this time and enjoyed the trip.

We got the barge tied up at Oakland Dock and Warehouse and then went on over to SF and tied up the boat at Pier 3. It was late at night by the time we got tied up and I had decided that I wanted to get a room at my favorite hotel. I walked up the dock and onto the street to the hotel. What the "hell" my hotel was gone. It was now a parking lot. I found out later that the Mayor had caused the building to be torn down because she owned the building behind the hotel and wanted to see out onto the Bay. That Mayor is now a left wing Democrat Senator in WDC. Nothing I could do but go back to the boat. I wonder what next is going to happen while I am on the next trip.

Chapter 7

Next morning there was a meeting in the office and I got my new orders.

I was to leave as soon as possible and run light to Anchorage, Alaska and wait for the Cuss#1 drilling ship to finish and get ready to be towed to SF. We went to the fuel dock and topped off the diesel fuel. Then we topped off the fresh water and the lube oil. The cook had loaded up on stores while we were at Pier 3.

We had a favorable weather report so maybe we will have a nice ride on up the coast. Sure did, all the way to the Columbia River and then a Northerly blew in and the ocean got 'snotty' in a hurry. As soon as it became apparent that we were in for it we all turned to and got the storm windows up. Good thing we did as the seas were up to 28ft and rolling on top for the next 4 days. We could not run at top speed and it would be a long run up to Trading Bay. I was hoping to get to Anchorage in time to let the crew off for a while. The water was coming over the bow in solid sheets and going all the way over the house. I was necessary to turn on the radar and the visibility was less than 300 ft. Oh well! Got to earn our pay. Sure glad Johnny was the cook. There have been times when in rough weather that all we could expect for chow would be cold sandwiches. Johnny always had something hot and lots of coffee.

We, at last, turned the corner and headed up the Bay. There was a 14knot ebb tide and so it was slow going even at full throttle. It was nice to be in calm water and no fog. The storm windows came down and they were stowed away for next time they were needed. We made it on up to the dock at Anchorage and got tied up and all secure. I told the crew that they could go on into town if they wanted. In just a little while I was all by myself and it was sure quiet. The tide falls and rises as much as 30ft. up here so it was important to check the lines often. Every 30 minutes on the ebb and each hour on the flood. I had my hands full all night. The crew came back early morning and I hit the sack.

I know of one boat that had not checked the lines as they should have and they became so tight that the boat actually started to rise up out of the water on the side next to the dock. The forward cleat came loose on the dock and came flying threw the air like a rocket and damaged the boat. The stern line had to be cut with a fire ax. Cutting a line that is fetched up so tight can cause a person to be hurt. As it was in that case a man was badly injured.

It would have been a lot easier if the boat crew had done their job and checked the lines.

There are lots of things that can happen when we go to town. Sometimes it gets real serious but usually it is just fun and the men have a good time. One night up in Anchorage all the crew was in a bar and having a good time playing pool and swapping tales. Some of the guys liked to dance and there were "ladies" to dance with. One of them took a liking to Frank and offered to give him a good time etc. She had said only $50 for a quicky and he told her to get lost and leave me alone. Well she was sure she could get him with the offer of $50 for all night. Anyhow this kept up all evening and each time she offered the price got lower. As we were heading out the door she grabbed him and said " a six pack of beer?". We got him out of there and safely onto the boat.

Bill, the engineer , and I had a contest going of pool playing. Every time that we could we played and over time we just about broke even. We played in SF, Anchorage, Portland, Guam, Manila, Hawaii, and many other places.

At last the Cuss#1 was ready for sea. We had moved down closer to her and were anchored so that we could be able to hook up quick. The tides are a big factor as they run so fast and we wanted to make our tie up on the slack water. The tide slacked and the Cuss#1 said let's go so hook up we did and we were underway just as the tide started to ebb. Everything went well as we were going on down the bay and it looked as though it was going to be a good tow. When we turned the corner and headed on our course to SF and the tide did not affect us now that we were out into the ocean the tow started to act up. It would seem to settle down and all of a sudden it would take off and run first one way and the next time it might run the other way. We had about 1800feet of tow line out and so when the ship would run out as far as it could go it was way out there and caused our boat to vibrate and shudder. Had to slow down and get the tow back in line and then speed up slowly and hope all would go well. The tow would do just fine for a while and then away it would go again. Maybe this time it would take off in the other direction and it was a good thing that we had the whole ocean to ourselves with no other traffic. The only other traffic was another tug and tow a few miles astern us. This other tug had another drill ship in tow. I called him on the radio and asked him how he was doing. He said ' I have never had a tow that was so erratic in all my life. Can not keep it behind me."

There must be some reason for the crazy runs and so I started to see if I could figure out a way to correct it. I changed rpms and went slow and fast and half speed but nothing seemed to help. I called the other tow in about 24hrs. and he had only made 1 mile over the bottom in all that time.

I heaved up wire with the hope that maybe a shorter wire would help. Believe it or not it did help but had to lower the rpms and go at a slower speed. Running on a short wire is dangerous but so long as the weather would hold and not blow up we could make do. We could only make about 5 knots and it was going to take a long time to get to SF. Called the other tow and told him and he was real happy to hear that and so he shorten up and slowed down and prepared for a long trip home.

It was necessary to keep a constant watch on the tow and the towline and one more time the small line on the wire proved that it was possible to observe any slipping of the wire. Sure glad that I had put out 2 shots of chain because running on a short wire the wire can fetch up and without the extra chain the line could part. The extra chain held the wire down and kept it from becoming too tight.

Three weeks later we at last made it into SF. The weather had held so there were no problems.

Chapter 8

We were told to take some RR and rest as they had a big deal coming up for us so we went home and kicked back for a while. Actually we did have some time at home. They did not even call me for a month. I was beginning to think that they were ticked off because we took extra time to bring those drill ships into harbor. Not so, they did have a big deal coming up. We were all going over to the coast and do some fishing. The camper was all loaded and the kids were all excited and ready and the phone rang! Yep you guessed it, report to the boat at 0700 in 2 days. Such is the life of a towboat man.

I got down to the office and they gave me my orders. Take on stores, fuel, and water and lube. oil and check everything that we might need for a long trip. We were to sail in 2days. We were to run light all the way to Jacksonville Fla. Pick up a tow and come back to Galveston, Tex. and pick up another tow . That meant that we would have two barges to tow back to SF. We had a good trip and going through the Panama

Canal was real easy and we went through with a ship so there was no holdup.

About three days out of SF we were having great weather with only light airs and flat calm. I was on duty in the wheelhouse and since we were not towing and just running along I put the steering into automatic and leaned back and sort of just took it easy. There are not many times that a guy can relax but without a tow I took advantage of it and guess I was thinking about home or what ever when " up came something out of the ocean" right in front of the boat and not more than 200yards away. At 10knots we were closing fast and being on automatic steering it was not possible to just come left or right without first putting the steering back into manual. This takes a few seconds for it to engage and it seemed as though it would not be quick enough but it did and since I had already slowed down I was able to come hard left and there was not more than 10feet between the boat and the object when we passed. The object turned out to be a Saturn Booster. I was able to read the letters U.N. These letters were about 6feet long, so that told me that the thing was coming about 12 feet plus the top of it at 10feet or around 22 feet out of the water. The whole lettering said United States, so at 6feet per letter plus the bottom of it would put the thing over 75feet and maybe more.

[We sure were lucky that I was at full attention and watching closely.]

I made a call to the Coast Guard and reported the sighting and they told me to standby and await further orders. In less than 2 minutes here came 2 fighter planes and they let me know to stay dead in the water until they could check things over. They did not have to tell me twice as they were real intimidating and looked like they meant business. It turned out that the Russians were looking for the booster too. They told me that we could proceed and as I was preparing to get underway I could see Navy ships coming. I guess they must have picked the booster up and loaded it onto a ship but I had an ETA in Panama and could not stay and watch.

The cook came up and let me know that dinner will be late. He had lost everything when I had come hard left in order to miss the booster. The food had fallen off the counter and onto the deck. All I could do was to say [do the best that you can]. He fixed a good meal and we ate OK.

The weather held and we had a good trip on down to Panama. We arrived at Balboa at about 0400 and waited for our turn. A ship was to go through and we were to get in behind her and go through with her. That way they did not have to fill the dock and empty it twice. They charged us the same as though we had gone through by ourselves so they made money on us for sure. We had finished with the Balboa locks and went on to Gatun Lake. It was going to be several hours in order to go through the Cristobal locks so we dropped the hook and went swimming. It must have been 100 degrees and real muggy so the swim felt good. Finally got the call to go through the locks and we were all done in about 2hours. Next thing was to get fuel so we went to pier 16 and fueled up. We also took on stores and water and I made sure that the fuel did not come off the bottom of their tank. Then it was off on the run to Jacksonville, Florida.

Since we were running light with no tow I came in real close to the Yucatan Pennisula because I wanted to see the white pristine beaches. They sure did not look the way I had hoped. Some of them were covered with Plastic bottles and Styrofoam cups etc. Anyhow I was glad to see the green trees and I tried to overlook the rest of the mess. Turned to the right and headed for Florida.

Got over to Florida and picked up a small barge and headed back to Galveston for the other barge. We got underway before the sun came up. It comes up out of the ocean on the east coast so we say [no wonder those folks are strange]. There was a wind blowing and a big sea was forming so I was glad to get underway and maybe get around the corner before it gets real snotty. We made it without much trouble and when we headed for Galveston the weather was much better. We got to the sea buoy in the afternoon and I was glad for that as there was a lot of traffic in the seaway. Tied up the small barge and went for the other one. It turned out to be one big piece of equipment and was the size of a football field and drew 25feet of water. Nine men were to ride on the barge. There were nice living quarters on board with all the necessities. The galley was bigger than most in houses and there were big freezers and refrigerators and one guy was to be the head cook but they could take turns if they wanted. Most of the men were so busy doing repairs and getting the barge ready for a big job that was coming up that they did not do much cooking.

First thing was to meet those men and lay down some towing rules. I called for a meeting and they all came onto the tug and we talked. They were all trained and were professional repairmen and engineers but towing was not their game. I made it clear to them that what they do back there on the barge could make or break the trip and could possibly cost them their lives. We set up a radio code and signals with hand held flags. We had CB radios as well as the Marine Radios and they were shown how to use each of them. They all ready knew but I did not want to take a chance. It could be too late to learn in an emergency. A big ,tall guy got up to say something. He turned out to be the head welder. "Don't panic if you see what looks like a fire as we have a lot of welding and cutting to do". Sure glad that he said something about that as it turned out that sometimes there was a big lot of fire coming from the barge because of their work. There were times that they worked at night and that made it look like the 4th of July. They were to have a regular check on the tow line and the cleats, and I said every hour and don't fail. The tow line was to be about 1800feet long so that put the barge a long ways back there. Also they were to keep a daily log on what was going on.

The barge was to be used as a crane barge and could lift 500 tons. They were to repair the crane and have it ready to use when we got to Port Hueneme. That Port is about halfway between LA and Santa Barbara and is a Military port. The next year I saw that same barge up in Alaska working in the oil drilling.

We were to take fuel from the barge so we went through the steps in order to take on the fuel without a slip up. We could run for about 30 days without running out but we would be sniffing the bottoms and so we always looked for fuel after two weeks. The weather may be OK , or it could be days before it would be possible to do the job. It was, or could be, a real nervous time. We had to fuel 4 times on this trip and each time was a real trial for us as well as for the men on the barge. One slip for one of those guys could be fatal. Each man had to put on a life jacket and the man on the front had a line attached to him , just in case. Slow down was the order for the day and think about each step. The deck of the barge was 20feet from the water.

The ocean was flat and the running time on this load of fuel had been 2 weeks so " now hear this fuel time ... all hands on deck". There was plenty of water under the boat so the tow-line could be safe from hanging up on the bottom but still had to heave up the wire. Winching up 1000ft of wire took a while and some of the guys got coffee and a bite to eat. When the barge was close enough we threw a line up to the guys on the barge and they made it fast onto the fuel hose. Then we heaved up on the line and got the fuel hose onto the boat and into the fill hole and started to fill.

It took about 8hrs. to fill up and we kept a watch on the weather. We finished the job and got everything secured and started to run out wire when the look-out reported " wind coming and building up off the port side".

In less than 2hrs the seas had grown and we were in for a blow. We had a full load of fuel and the boat rode well. Sure were " looked after".

The next time that we fueled we were not so "lucky" and we had to stop and secure with only enough fuel to run 2weeks total. By the time that we got secure on that fill-up the seas were running over the stern and it was getting rough. That blow only lasted a few days and the ocean laid down so here we go again with the fueling. That time we were able to take a full load and were in good shape.

The men on the barge had been ordered to make sure that everything was secured and lashed down so that gear could not run loose and cause trouble.

There was no more gripping about stowing and securing gear. One of the men had come right out of Nebraska and of course knew all about the ocean. He made the remark that "we are 20ft up from the water and are safe" Well he sure got a lesson when the sea was coming up and over the barge. The men were quick to learn and did a good job. They had a great deal of work to do and they worked every day that they could.

The weather turned out real calm and we were just more or less taking it easy and doing the regular details that were necessary.

One of the deckhands and the engineer were in the wheelhouse just looking at the dolphins and the birds and sea.

Pat said "I wonder how much 5/16 chain we have on board? "

I replied "That there should be plenty as we have not used much up until now".

Next thing he wanted to know whether we needed all of the 3/4inch plywood? We only needed 1 and a half sheets so I said " no, not all of it but we want to take care of what we do have".

"Would it be OK if I could have a couple small pieces?" he asked.

About this time I was wondering what this guy had in mind but decided to keep my mouth shut and watch what he was doing. The engineer was sitting there and taking it all in but I noticed that he had a smirk on his face so he had a idea what was going to happen.

Two days went by and we were making good speed and everything was as should be and here came Pat.

"Good morning Cap. How do you like these"? He showed me 2 real nice slingshots that he had made out of 3/4inch plywood.

"What are you going to use for ammunition"? He had a sack of 5/16 chain that he had cut the links into and they made perfect shots.

That seaman had it all figured out and out the hatch he went and took aim at a stick that was near the boat and almost hit it. Soon it was to become a regular contest and all the men got into the act. We made up a list of the men and marked down the hits and misses. The targets varied and it could be flotsam, sticks, flying fish, birds or anything else in the area.

It became apparent to me , that seaman has something on the ball. I started to watch him closer and pegged him for extra duty. He was given more responsibility and also made sure that he was to spend time in the wheelhouse learning more. His problem was that he wanted to make money by putting in extra time doing "chores" such as painting etc. I made him do as he was told and made him spend time in the wheelhouse sorting charts, or figuring out our speed etc. He soon got the message and learned really quick and well. He sailed with me for the next 2years and became one of the best mates that a skipper could have. That same man got a command of his own at last and is doing well. Just think what a slingshot could lead into.

I thought about the fish that people spend $1000's of dollars to catch and we were right in the area where the fish are. There were two lengths of ¾ inch pipe on board and they would make real good line out riggers. So I rigged them outboard on each side off the Texas deck and ran two lines from them, one long line and one short line. Pat came up and caught me. "well I'll be damned, look what the Capt is up to". He jumped right in and helped me finish the set-up. Now we had slingshots and fishing outriggers. I know that the men could have those diversions and still do their jobs so to shooting and fishing we went. By the way, the speed that we were going was 3 knots and that was the speed for trolling for a lot of fish. I knew, because I had just read an article in one of the various magazines on board, and I said to myself, why not? The first day we sure caught a lot of fish. A few Mahi mahi and some others. One day I hooked into a Marlin and when he came up out of the water he looked to be 20feet long but we lost him as he broke the line. We could not stop, slow down or change course so sometimes we would get tangled up in the tow line. Some of the people around the dock saw the line wrapped around the towline and I am sure that they thought that we had run over someone's fishing line. We did not tell them any different.

It was necessary to make repairs and do some maintenance in the engine room and it was all done without shutting down the engines. Each man had ear covers to keep out some of the noise but it was still necessary to use hand signals etc. There were lots of finger pointing, waving, and sometimes pushing. It was so hot down there that after using a wrench it was dropped into a bucket of water to stay cool. Laying a tool onto the deck would be a no....no and if you wanted to get someone's goat try it. Each man would work 30 minutes and then he would go top-side for 30 in order to cool down.

The fishing was great and we put fillets in the freezer. We had fresh fish on the menu, but most of it was to take home. One of the men had been born and raised in the Islands and he thought that the fresh heart of the Mahi-Mahi was a treat. He would take out the heart and eat it raw, Yuk! He was a real good sailor though so we overlooked that. Many fish change color as soon as they are removed from the water but the Mahi-Mahi would also go from the most beautiful colors to plain old brown as soon as it died. They are some of the best eating fish in the ocean.

Chapter 9

We had been at sea 17 days when at last we got in sight of Panama. Made radio contact and was told to slow down and that it would be 3 days before we could make it into the locks. Some times there is lots of traffic and each ship had to take their turns. We were particularly at risk because of the size of the barge. The barge was so big that it barely fit into the locks. Sure glad that we could get into them as it would be 7800 miles around. We had to sit out in the ocean until they told us to come on in and go through. It was an expensive business to use the canal and cost us plenty.

It was necessary to let go of the barge and get astern of it and push it through the locks. No big deal but it took a ½ day longer. After we got through we had to set up a regular tow and make it to Mira Flores and repeat the pushing routine. Took us almost 2 days to get to the other side.

We got through the last locks about dark and headed for the fuel docks to top off. Of course they were closed so we waited until morning and topped off the boat and took on about 50,000 gals onto the barge. Sure will be nice to get back to sea. Diesel was 10 to 15cents per gallon but it cost plenty to fill up. The boat held 84,000 gals and the barge had a capacity of 100,000gals.

At last we were on the Pacific Ocean. The ocean was flat calm and the going was a sailor's dream. We had a few repairs to do on the engine but most of the work was just the normal stuff. It was so flat that it was a good time to break out the lines and other gear that is stored in the compartment that is in the after deck on the stern. The hatch cover is on the deck and is open to any water that gets onto boat. " Where is the small line and is the deck cover aft dogged down"? The men knew what I meant and more than one time one of them would have to go see. Better safe than sorry. There was one boat that did not pay attention and as a result the boat was swamped and all hands went down with it.

Pat …"put all the lines that you can onto the deck to dry out and check all the straps and other metal gear for rust". The hatch was left open but only if someone was on deck . He organized the crew and got the work done in a hurry. It was not necessary to tell him to look over the other gear that is on the after deck. He made a good report and logged the info. Also he put into the log that the hatch cover was dogged down and checked by 2 other crewmen before he left.

The fishing lines had been put out and we were catching lots of fish as there seemed to be more fish in the Pacific Ocean. We caught skip-jack, tuna, bonita, mahi-mahi and others. We had some big fish on but were not able to bring them in. Ended up with more line around the tow line. When we got in we had 50# of fillets per man.

Had to take on fuel again and were able to top off as the weather was perfect and the ocean calm.

Started to have trouble with the steering again so we had to jury rig the system in order to keep going. The engineer held lessons on what to do to operate the steering by hand. We wanted to make it into Port Hueneme and do the repair there. We got abeam of Mexico and went into Acapulco and into the little bay there and came alongside the barge to make some quick repairs. We had been careful to remove all the fishing gear and put it all away out of sight. Oh! Oh! Here comes the famous "federales". Those guys are the Mexican Police and they are a bunch of leaches. They accused us of fishing in their waters and wanted to arrest us. I waved some money in their faces and the head honcho said "Capitan' put more money in the sombrero". I added a little and once more he said " More money in the sombrero" so once again I added a little and this time he let me know not to stay much longer. "Adios". It cost the boat $300 dollars for that caper.

We got underway again and we were glad to be back out to sea.

Started up the lessons again to learn how to steer by hand.

The engineer came up with the idea of using the PA system to transfer the orders from the wheelhouse to the man on the control in the engine room. Show several people what to do. It turned out that Joe caught on the best. Now we had to try the PA system to see whether it would really work.

I said over the system "come to the left". There was so much noise in the engine room that the orders could not be heard or understood.

Pat came up with " let's try whistling" and since I did not understand his reasoning I told him " to quit being a wise ass, that this is very serious.".

His reply was "just listen, and I don't need to be told how serious this is". He whistled once, then twice, and then three times, once for left, two for right and three times for mid-ship. OK try it. Even with all the noise in the engine room the signals could be heard easily. So now if the steering was to fail using the wheelhouse controls we would be able to maneuver , with the use of the whistles.

We kept on going and at last we got sight of Port Hueneme so I called in our ETA and asked for a tug to stand by until we got tied up at the dock. Everything went along real well and so I got permission to stay where we were until the repairs could be done. It took us 2 days to get them done and then we went over to the fuel dock and topped off again. We should not have to take on any more fuel for this trip. It was a real calm ocean that we sailed out into and made a fast trip up to SF. Sure good to see the sea buoy that marks the entrance to the channel for SF. The tide was just starting to flood so we were on our way to the Golden Gate Bridge in a hurry. No fog either and it was as though we were being welcomed home in grand style.

It had taken 4 months and 10 days to make the trip and the crew was glad to get paid off and head for home. Each man had a box of fish to take with them and the ones that lived a long way from SF passed their fish off to someone that lived closer. We had no ice chests and a plain box would get ripe before long. As soon as I could get the paper work done, away I went for home.

Chapter 10

Sure nice to be with the family and this time we did not fool around and got things in the camper and headed for the coast for some laying around and some diving and fishing. The kids were able to get some of their own abalone and we had great feeds while at the camp. We really enjoyed the times that we had together at the coast and they refer to those times when ever we see each other now. One of the best things was that there was no telephone and no way to talk to me from the office. We stayed over at the coast for about 10 days and I knew that as soon as I was home the phone would start ringing. Sure enough the phone was doing it's "ding a ling" almost as soon as I opened the door.

The orders were to report in two days to Pier 3 and the Tug Samson. At least I had time to unload the camper and get things squared away. We had quite a few abalone to clean and so on. Also I had time to look the place over and see the homestead. There were cows, horses, chickens, pigs, ducks, and other critters that the kids and the wife took care of. The family had a large garden and all hands helped with that. The old saying is that " sailors all want a dirt farm way away from the sea ". Well we sure did. There was almost no bitching or gripping about all the things that had to be done. It was common to have as many kids at our table that would double the population of the household. Our place was the meeting place from 20 miles around. Some of them stayed over night and many times the parents would call to see if their little darlings were at our house. We put up with no bad manners or anything that was not right. The kids, ours and the visitors, were respectful and behaved themselves well. There was an occasional fight but in those days we figured that it was just growing up. We loved them all and even today they call up to say howdy and pass the time of day.

I got to SF and reported in. Why don't you answer your phone? I did not say that we had been camping. Hell, getting away was the only way to get some time off. A few years later I ended up buying a ranch up north that had no phone or electricity and I could really hide away. It was 40 miles from town and the nearest neighbor was 4 miles away. We all liked our jobs but sometimes we wanted some time off. Oh, well the pay was good.

Chapter 11

This time my orders were to take a barge load of equipment over to Hawaii. The whole deck was full of tractors, loaders, graders and some other small stuff that is used in road building. It was necessary to weld hold downs onto the deck in order to secure everything. Took us 3 days to get all the equipment so that it could be safe.

We finally got underway and on to Hawaii. We had a good trip and everything rode well on the barge. This time we had no time for fishing and anyhow we were going too fast for trolling. As we got close I reported our ETA and they said take the barge to Barbours Point and tie it up there at dock C. Go to the fuel dock and top off and take on what stores that we will need. They had not told me what was the next move, so we did load up on stores.

Tie up near the #106 barge and wait for it to be unloaded and when it is take it to SF. It took 2 days for the barge to be ready for sea. We got some of the work done on the boat , such as some painting, and greasing of the winches and other things that are always needed. At last it was ready and we made up a tow and were set to go. I called in and reported that we were ready to depart and the office at the Traffic Center said to stand by until the equipment barge passes and is in the clear. Here it came and with a Jap tug towing. Guess it is another case of our government giving away our stuff. That Jap did not even dip her colors but did give us the danger signal in order to show off.

We got underway and headed for SF.

The trip to SF was fast and we got tied up at pier 3. The radio started to transmit and I was told to report to the office and as soon as things were squared away on the boat I went there and was not prepared for what I heard.

There were several men in the office and I was introduced all around. Four of the men were from the towing industry and there was one man from the GOV'T. It made me feel a little uneasy with all that brass around but I knew that something was up.

They were concerned about getting supplies delivered to Viet Nam with the use of Tugs and Barges. The barges were to be loaded and then towed over to Viet Nam and in some cases the tug was to stand by until they were unloaded and towed back to Manila. While waiting in Viet Nam for the barge the tug was to do ship work or what ever else that was needed. At Manila there were loaded barges ready to be towed back to Viet Nam. These barges were loaded with every thing from ammo to equipment etc. They wanted to know what I thought about it. All that I could tell them was that it was not going to be a picnic and would take constant awareness and caution. I wanted some weapons and ammo on board the tug and of course that went over like a lead balloon. It is odd that people that are unable to fire a weapon or know nothing about protection are the one's that set policy. I suggested that the men would be paid hazardous duty pay. The eyebrows came up on that idea also. At least they heard from me.

I did not know what they were thinking but 2 weeks went by and they kept me at the dock doing some maintenance work and painting. During this time at the dock several people that I knew had gone into the office and after a while they got into their cars and drove away. After another week they told me to go on home and that they would call me. It was nice to be home and after about a week I got to thinking that maybe they had forgotten me. No such luck because "ding-a-ling" and they said to be at the office at 0800.

We had been invited to a big party and dance and were looking forward to a really good time but with me having to be at the office first thing in the morning we did not go. Oh, well, the life of a towboat man.

Chapter 12

I left for the City at 0600. Leaving early I could beat some of the traffic and not have to drive fast. I took about 1hr. and 15min. to get to there. As soon as I got there I went right to the office.

"Good morning Capt. Have a cup of coffee." I wondered what now.

There was at least 45mins of small talk and yakaty yak and I began to feel uncomfortable. At last in walked that same gov't man that had been at the first meeting.

He started out by saying that "we have reviewed our first meeting and have come to the conclusion that we want you to be our man for the Manila to Viet Nam run". I just sat there and did not say anything. He said "hello are you with us?" At last I came to and told him that I was ready to do my part. He said " thank you and God Bless".

I got my orders and was to fly to Hawaii. I was to be met by a company man and he was to take me to the boat. The boat was fairly new and looked like a good one. None of the crew was on board except for the engineer and he was a man that I had known from another boat and I knew that he was a real good one. He and I did our own cooking for the first 2 days and then here came the crew. I knew most of them from other trips and my written orders read to converse with each man and determine whether or not they had any reservations about this trip.

They were all tug men and knew their jobs. The cook was an old friend of mine and I knew that he was an excellent cook.

We were told that the barge would not be ready for two days so that gave us time to check everything over and make sure that we were ready for sea and a long trip. We topped off the fuel, lube oil and the fresh water. All the charts were on board for a change. The second mate charted the first 24hours and had all in order. This would be a trial run for the gov't and the company and we wanted to do it right.

The barge was a big one and it probably would fit into a football field but maybe not. It looked as though it would tow OK and we put out 2 shots of chain and that proved to be a sound move as we did hit some rough seas. The barge was loaded with every machine that was used in a machine shop and had a house over every bit of it. It looked as though the house would cause the barge to act like a great big sail and make the tow wander but it did not and towed real well. The machines were all new and up to date. There were milling machines, lathes, drill presses, welding and forge equipment, and all the tools needed in order to build most anything. No wonder this war was costing so much money. It turned out that all this was left over there when we pulled out of the war.

The trip from Hawaii to Manila was a long one and had a lot of extra stuff to do. Had to do a lot of repairs and adjustments to the engine dept.

One of the bilge pumps needed to be replaced but we repaired it and got it running. I have to make sure to get a replacement pump and keep it on hand for future use. We could be in a world of hurt if the pumps are not working.

It was the next day that the RPM reading was fluctuating and after awhile they went down so here we go again! Had to change fuel filters and that meant that it was necessary to stop the engine and look out for the barge. Actually this was a good thing to have this happen on the way to Hawaii and not on the way to Viet Nam. Also we can get more filters in Manila.

The weather report was not very encouraging. They reported that the weather is turning for the worse and that we could expect heavy winds. Ordered the storm windows to be put up. The wind was building fast and before the men could finish the job it was necessary to attach a safety line to each man and even then it became real dangerous. The mate was an old hand and knew to keep the sheets tight alongside the bulkhead and work them up slowly. One of the men was new to this business of storm windows and was trying to do it right and had not listened to the mate. "Get that sheet down and leave it down until I call for it." The warning was too late and the sheet was caught in the wind and sailed out over the side. It could have caught the deckhand and took him over the side. Lesson learned and things turned out OK. We had extra sheets so all the windows were covered. We clocked the winds at 90 miles per hour and water was coming over in solid waves. Reduced the RPM and just kept the boat into the wind but our speed was down to nothing.

Four of the men were sitting down in the mess room talking and having coffee and trying not to worry about the storm. The boat was rolling badly and solid water was clear up 4feet on the sides as she rolled. Bill hollered out " if you do that again Joe, I will punch you out". Joe had no idea what Bill was upset about and told him so. Well as soon as the boat rolled again the same thing happened and Bill came unglued. Frank was sitting on the side and knew what was happening so he said " take it easy Bill and pretty soon the same thing will happen again. Keep your eye on Joe and watch real careful and see what he does". The boat took another big roll and sure enough the same thing happened. Joe was just sitting there and Bill was once again splattered with water. " Does that taste like salt water Bill?" He admitted that it did and said so " sorry Joe".

Each time the boat rolled the water was forced through the keyhole in the hatch on the weather deck and was sent across the mess room with speed and volume and Joe was sitting in the wrong spot. We all pulled Bill's leg on that one.

We crossed the dateline and the second mate was the only one that had not ever crossed it so he was elected to be the fall guy for the day. We made him put on a wig and sing a song for all hands. I think it was Mary Had a Little Lamb or something like that. Anyhow we had fun.

The wind calmed down at last and sure was good to get those storm windows down and stored away.

The flying fish at last showed up and put on their show for us. Some of them could fly the length of the boat and pass us before dropping back into the water. Each morning Johnny the cook, would look on the main weather deck and gather up flying fish and shrimp that had landed on the deck. He would cook them and boil potatoes for breakfast. He and I would always enjoy that breakfast, but most of the other men wanted eggs, bacon etc.

We got close to Manila and I called their Traffic Center and they said that they would have a pilot ready when we were ready to go into the harbor. We were to anchor out and they would show us where to drop the hook. Liberty boats made frequent runs out to the ships that were in the anchorage so it was possible to go ashore. I had to go into the office and have a meeting. The crew could go but only 2 or 3 at a time. It turned out that we would spend a week there so everyone had a chance to see Manila.

Most of the people were friendly and did not cause any trouble. The older ones in particular remember the Jap occupation and all the horrible things that they had done during the War. We came in and saved their country and kicked out the Jap invaders.

One of the things that I did was to hire a taxi service. The driver and owner is named Dan. I do not know his real name but a lot of the people used Dan or Danny as a name that we could pronounce and it worked out for the most part. Another name that was popular was Joe. Joe was always along in the cab because he was the money changer and could always exchange money for us at a higher rate than any of the "official" money exchangers. As far as Dan was concerned we had his cab and would have been upset if we were to use any other cab. How he knew when we came in to the harbor was something that was a mystery to me. He would be right at the dock and it made no difference which dock we came into. "Hi boat- Hi boat" and he would be jumping up and down to make sure that we saw him. It got so that the whole crew would look for him each time that we came in." There he is" one of the guys would shout and everyone would try to see him. One time we were still a mile off the dock and one of the crew said "I see him". It actually became a contest as to who could see him first.

The fact that we had a taxi was a big help to the boat. Not only that we did not have to look for a cab but more important was that he could be trusted. His cab was painted in very bright colors and shined and was always clean. All of the taxis liked to honk their horns when they were on the road and some times the noise was deafening but they could sure drive. Many times they would be going 6 abreast on a 4 abreast road but I did not see any accidents.

It seems that no matter if the boat is new or older there are breakdowns. It was necessary to put a new part in the engine and so I got in touch with Danny the taxi guy and he said OK but you will have to go with me. Do not bring anybody else and that it will take between 2 or 3 hours to go and come back. The destination was way out in the jungle on a very narrow road. He turned at a driveway and about ¼ mile later there was ahead a large building. It looked completely out of place here in the jungle. I imagine that the building was left over from the war.

He told me to stay with him and do not wander around and I glued myself to him. The people that I saw all had weapons of some kind. There were pistols, carbines, machetes and they looked as though they knew how to use them. I believe that any outsider would have been killed, but they knew Danny. We went around several isles that were lined with shelves that were at least 8ft high and they were all stacked with thousands of parts. Danny knew his way around and soon he pointed about head high and there was the exact part that was needed. How he could find that was a mystery to me. Hell, if he got away from me I doubt that I could have found my way out of that building. He told me again to "stick close". He reached up and handed me the part. That part was just like holding a bomb, it seemed to me. I asked Dan if maybe he should be carrying it and he insisted that I carry it. The part weighed about 35lbs and was necessary to use both hands to balance it. I think that he wanted to have his hands free to use if it came to trouble. We made our way around all the isles and stuff and at last got to the exit. There was the biggest man I had seen in a long time at the door and in his hand was a 30caliber carbine with a 30 round clip. Danny paid him and we got to the taxi and I was sure glad when we were out on the road.

We did not have any trouble on the way back to the boat. I paid Danny for the part and it was so cheap that I gave him a nice tip.

We had to stand by and wait for our barge. It gave us time to spruce up the boat and check all the equipment. The barge that we were to take back to Viet Nam was loaded with ammo and weapons. There was an air-conditioner that was powered by a diesel engine and could run for 3 weeks on one fill up. The temperature in the barge could climb to excessive highs and the unit would be able to keep things within safe levels.

We topped off fuel and took on stores and we got more fuel filters.

Chapter 13

Our orders were , to leave in two days at 0800. I asked in the office if there was any reason that we had to wait until the posted departure time and he did not think that there was. It seemed to me that if we could leave without advertising the time we might be safer. Where we had to go there might be pirates and our cargo would be a prime target. We did not see any but we felt as though leaving quietly was a good idea.

We got within a mile of Viet Nam and here came a US gun boat and we were given an escort. They patrolled around us and we felt safe. How the Viet Cong enemy got on board the barge we will never know but they did. A troop of Marines had come on board us and since we had shortened up the tow wire the distance was just right for the Marine sharp shooters. It was not a good idea to shoot into the barge and those guys picked the enemy off and I did not see any strikes on the metal barge. The gun boat got some more of them in the water. It was not until later that we found out that one of them had a bomb but he had not set it. If it had blown the barge we would have surely been hurt.

We got our orders and we had to take an empty barge back to Manila. The barge was a fuel barge and was one of the big ones. Could hold about a million gallons.

We did not like to stay in Viet Nam very long as they always managed to have a job to do and of course we are the only ones to get it done. We had a ship to assist, a bunch of barges to move around, and several other misc. chores that we had to do. The barge that we were to take back to Manila was not quite unloaded and would not be finished for 2 more days. Oh well, nothing like being in the action. We had a detachment of Marines that stayed on board and they were relieved every 6 hours. At night they would come aboard and relieve the men and in so doing they always had some kind of drill as they sure were noisy. Not one of my crew ever said anything about the racket or complained because we knew that they were doing a good job and keeping us safe.

The barge was at last ready for sea and we made up a tow and away we went. It towed real well and after we got out into the open sea we "hooked it on" and made almost 10knots. The weather was calm and we could see in all directions clear to the end of the ocean. The curvature of the earth limited the distance that can be seen. Made it back to Manila and got tied up and the office told me to take 3 days and kick back and rest. Wow, what a surprise.

Some of the guys went into town and looked around and bought presents for their families and in general had a good time. None of the guys got drunk and caused any trouble and I am sure that it was a first. Sure made things easier for me. I got the paper work done and went to town myself.

Chapter 15

Manila was an interesting town and I enjoyed just watching the people. Someone was always trying to sell us Americans things. I say things because most of the stuff was just junk. At last a 'salesman' came to me and had just what every guy needs. He had the nicest set of water buffalo horns.

They were not just horns but also had some decoration on them. Anyhow we spent the next ½ hour haggling over the price and at last we made a deal. I had found out that his family was hungry and that his daughter was sick and the boy had no work and after all that I made a good purchase. My son has the horns even to this day. We spend a lot of time worrying about nothing compared to the poverty that those people suffer each day.

On board the boat was an armed guard that stayed until we sailed. One day there was a big disturbance and it seems that a person had come on board to do some work but he was not hired to do anything. He had come on board to steal. The guard had him up against the bulkhead and asked me if he wanted him shot. "Hell no just get him off the boat and be more careful". If that man had been shot the police would have made a "federal case" out of it and would have held the boat up for who knows how long. The thief had in his hands a toothbrush and some other toilet articles. They have very little and will steal "what-ever.

One of the men was late getting back to the boat. I did some inquiring as to what may have happened to him and was told that he was at a bar not too far into town. The guys had been at that bar and when they left he would not come with them. If we had not gone to get him he would have been robbed and probably killed as soon as the boat had put to sea. I told those guys that they should not have left him alone in the bar. "Come on Joe and Bill let's go get him".

We walked into the bar and there he was wrapped around one of the "ladies" and did not even see us come in. He was "three sheets to the wind and had lost his rudder". He told me to go to hell and that he was going to stay right there with that girl. I got his attention with a left tap and then lowered the boom with a hard right. Joe and Bill kept my back clear and I dragged Art out of the joint. We got him into the taxi and on to the boat. He was still out cold when we put him into one of the storage lockers and locked the door. The locker was big enough so that he could stand or lie down.

We got underway and headed out for another run to Viet Nam. This time we had a barge that was loaded with more machinery. It towed well and we were able to keep the RPMs up and made good speed. The weather was fine and the flying fish were really thick. I think that they like it when a boat is moving along fast with "a bone in her teeth".

I made sure that Art was sober and OK. He told me how sorry he was and thanked us for not letting him stay. Nice speech but he will be watched from now on.

The next day the wind hauled around and the sea started to pick up and we had to slow down. We got into Viet Nam OK and were told that we were to go back to Manila with no tow. It seemed that things were slowing down in the war. There was not the activity around the area and that fuel barge was not unloaded yet. Normally we would be towing the empties back to Manila to be loaded up again.

Sure enough the wind kept on building and the seas were terrible. The storm windows were installed in time to save the windows. The weather report said mariners alert and warning that a hurricane is coming. We battened down all the hatches and secured all that we could. The temperature kept rising and soon it was 120 degrees in the mess room and 134 in the engine room. These boats did not have air conditioning. We had to slow down and even then we were taking water over the house. Had to make sure to run into the waves and not get down into the trough.

All we could do was to stay on manual control and rev. up or lower rpms as needed. No chance to take a relief. The first mate and I did the steering and engine control. The engineer was down in the engine room checking and rechecking and everything was running real well so I told one of the men to tell him to come out of there. He got coffee in the mess and headed for the wheelhouse. It was better to have him out of the engine room and up with us. He made checks every half hour and looked things over. We all agreed that taking the time to look things over and make any repairs at the dock and where it was calm had been a good idea.

We were taking water into the engine room each time that the seas came over the house. The water entered at the small vent stack forward of the main stack. Not much but any made us uneasy. The pumps kept right on working so there was not any build up of water. The hatch on the weather deck aft did not leak even though it was under water almost all the time. It seemed that there was water seeping in from somewhere all the time during heavy weather.

The sea had built up and the small waves were only 20 feet high but the big ones were 40 to 60 feet or so. These tugs are sure tough and can be depended upon. Of course they had to be sailed and not just run. This lasted about 48 hours and at last the wind started to abate and the sea was getting less angry and we were even able to take a shot and see what our position was. We were 2 days from Manila so actually we had lost way during the blow.

We had lost our small boat and the control unit was gone from the Texas deck. The overall boat was in good shape. Sure fortunate that we had one of these tough tug boats.

We got in close to Manila and made a report as to our position and condition and they told us to dock at the fuel dock and then take on stores etc. for a long trip. They had a real nice small boat for us and they replaced the control unit so we were back to normal. The storm and so on was all contained in my written report.

Most of the men got mail from home. One poor guy was told by his wife that no longer is she going to stay home while he was "playing around on the ocean". Guess she must have been playing around at home.

Next morning I went to our local office and made my report and got our new orders. Go to Guam and take a tow to SF. We were to run to Guam as soon as we could leave. It was nice to be running in friendly waters for a change. There were no pirates in these waters as far as I could find out.

It was not necessary to go looking for any of the crew before we left. Guess they learned a lesson about leaving the girlies on the beach and putting the boat first

Chapter 16

We had left for Guam within 24 hours and charted a course straight for there. It was a 1600 mile run and the sea was calm for the most part. It was great to be able to relax a little and actually got some sleep.

Two of the men said that they would like to do all the extra work that they could so I told the mate to put them to work. He and I took a tour and decided what projects needed to be done. Any work over 8 hours was overtime and those guys wanted to make as much as they possibly could in order to have a real good payoff at the end of the trip. Both of them had wives and kids at home and the work had to be done. We were all to receive "hazard pay" for the time in the war zone and that will be a nice addition to the regular check.

The weather was calm and the sea was flat so they started chipping and painting up forward. It always makes a noise that can be heard through out the boat when that is happening. Also the noise echoes into the water and it was no more than 10 min. after it started than here came the porpoises. They would swim alongside and always on the starboard side only. Sometimes they were no more than 2 feet from the hull and were very visible. One came each day and it was easy to distinguish him because of the scars that were on both of his sides and back. On days that no chipping was going on they would not come up to the boat. We could see them off in the distance but not alongside. I went down to the main deck and leaned over and gently banged my cup on the side and in a few minutes here came "scars". He saw me and rolled and looked and then splashed water at me. I think that he really liked the company and just wanted to say hello.

It took us 5 days to get to Guam and the wind was up and it was raining. I called for longshoremen but there were none available so I tied up at the first dock. Sure as hell we had to move later because we were in the wrong spot. The dock hands were all Porto Ricans and they would not work in the rain, poor little wimps. The Guam natives worked for the gov't, drove taxis or worked in construction.

The radio started up and I was told to come to the office. I answered " OK but where is the office?" He said "see that small building on the dock right ahead of you? If you get lost we will come and get you!" Kind of got my chain rattled and hoped that everyone else that I had to deal with was a little nicer.

I got the hint and took off for that little building. Inside was one of the fattest men I had ever seen. He took off his headset and said "sit down". He handed me a set of blue prints and told me to study them and get that boat ready for sea. Take all the time that you will need. Talk to a man named Hernandez and he will have the yard and equipment for you. " that is all good luck". That fat man was another case of someone with a little job but thinks he is really something.

I took the plans and left the office and then I realized that I did not know anyone named Hernandez. Sure would not go back in and ask him.

Along in the afternoon a guy was on the dock and wanted to talk to the Capt. He turned out to be Hernandez and we got started. First things first though so we had a cup of coffee. We got acquainted and I could see that we were going to get along fine.

He knew his job and the first thing he did was to put the tug up on the ways so we could check the hull and the rudder and we took off the wheel. The rudder was fixed in position at the mid ship position and tied down. The shaft packing gland was stuffed tight so it would not leak. He spent another day just checking everything until he and

I were happy with the results. He put the boat back into the water and started on the deck and house.

All the windows were boarded up and the hatches were all secured except one to be so we could gain entrance inside if needed. Towing a boat is a lot different than running one. It would be another week before we felt as though she is sea worthy.

One day he said that he did not have to drive taxi that night and to please come over for dinner. I said OK. I will pick you up and bring you back. That was fine with me as I had no idea where to go. His wife was an excellent cook and his three children were wonderful. After dinner and coffee he said "let's go". I got into his car and we started out but he turned the wrong way for the boat and I said so.

His reply was "I want to show you something". We went way out into the country and pulled into a driveway and parked next to a whole lot of other cars. I knew something was up but he was a nice guy so went along with him. We went into the building and I saw my first chicken fight. Of course they were all roosters and what a show. This is one of the big activities on the island. I lost $2.80 on the first fight but won $18 on the next one. Went home about even but it was a very interesting evening. He did better and made a fist full. I was the only non native there so I felt really privileged and I respect their culture.

A lot of people think that cock fights are awful and that it should be stopped. Well I say that we should let people have their cultures. We are all over the world trying to change them to our ways.

I am real tired of my tax money being used to change other countries to be just like us.

We got back to work and it was another week before the tug was ready for sea.

The tow line was made up to the boat and we were ready to put to sea and head for SF. Away we went and after we had gotten around the point we slipped wire and charted a course for the big city.

There was a little lump running but the tow was riding well and things looked to be in good shape.

About 2 days later the tow line parted and we were in trouble. It turned out that it was not reported or noticed for several hours and so we had to go on a hunt for the tow.

All hands on deck! That order was not welcomed at all but it was necessary to heave up the wire and get it out of the way and have a good lookout. I sent one of the seamen up the rigging and told him to hang on but look well.

I came around 180 degrees and headed back looking for that tug. The 2nd mate sure was not paying attention while on watch and we must have run for at least 2 hours before the break had been noticed. The wind had picked up and the sea was building and it was getting rough. That made everything that much tougher. I put the mate on the port side of the texas deck and the deckhand on the starboard side and told them to "quit your dam whining and look for that tug." The tug was sighted finally and now we have to get a line on her. A line had been spliced and ready to attach but with the seas as they were we could not get close enough. I told the mate to bring me a cup of coffee. The coffee came ok but the deckhand delivered it. I told the deckhand to get that mate up here,now! " When I tell you to bring coffee I mean you and not someone else. Take a shot and give me a report on our position." "I'm not on watch " was his reply.

Some guys never will learn when to keep their mouths shut and he got a lesson from me in a hurry.

If I had gone along with the position that he had calculated we would have had to run for a day or two to see the tug. Poor guy sure had to grow up.

We had to stand by and wait for the sea to lay down. Two days later along about 1200 I decided to take a chance to get up to the tug close enough to put the line on. Came bow on and the lead deckhand was able to get the line attached. The other end had been made fast onto the aft cleat and we were in business.

We were fairly close to Midway but on the east side of Kure Island was a nice calm bay that would work out real well for making up a proper tow. It was necessary to stay on the slow bell with the jury rig we had and also the tow was only about 500 ft to the stern of us and would not last long. Anyhow, to that island we went.

The tow line that had parted was inspected and we found out that the connection to the D-ring had rusted inside and had deteriorated and started to work loose and finally let go. Sure a good thing that we had another tow line on board. It looked to be in good shape and had not been used. The crew worked as hard as they could and did everything with care. The tow was all hooked up and we got underway in about 5 hours. I figured that the lack of attention and slacking on that watch had cost us about 6 days all together.

The mate sure got it " in the ringer" when we got to SF. Of course it did not look good on my record either.

We still had about 12 days to get to SF so I had lots of time to " chew ass". No more just standing watch. "where is the small line"? "is the shaft alley hatch dogged down"? " is there any water in the lazzarette"? There were other things that needed to be checked and either I or the mates would expect answers and I wanted all that logged in the book. This whole job was dangerous enough without getting lazy and not paying attention.

At last we could see the Golden Gate and she sure looked pretty. We had been gone and at sea most of the time for 7 months. Might get lucky and get some time off. Sure had a nice payoff. The wife received $400 per month as an allotment so I figured that there would be a whole bunch of bills to be paid. She had not charged a thing and owed no extra. I still am amazed at how she could manage on so little money.

She sold stuff off the ranch, vegetables, ducks, chickens, eggs and did without. She did not complain and did it out of love. How different than some of the things that most of the other men had to contend with. The kids turned out well because they had a good teacher.

Chapter 17

Oh well , back to sea.

I had almost a whole month off this time but one day here came the famous "ding-a-ling" so here I go again. Some of the men had a lot of trouble, waiting for the phone to ring but not I. The time that I spent at home was busy time for me. None of this waiting at some bar without family and loved ones around. We always had lots to talk about and one of the subjects that came up almost everyday was, could you find a way to stay closer so you could be home more. My reply would be, maybe or something like that. But it got me to thinking so we'll see.

The orders were to come to SF ASAP and we'll have your orders for you. I left for there in the morning and after parking and making sure that the tide book was on the dash I headed for the office. I left all my gear in the pickup and went down the dock empty handed. I always carried a monkey fist with a foot long line on it. This I had in my belt and was easy to get at. When I was parking etc. I had noticed a foreign ship tied up at the dock and about 100 feet from the pickup there was some movement behind a large truck parked and as I got close there were about 10 oriental men waiting for me. I really do not know what problem they had and I did not wait for them to explain. Out came the monkey fist and the first 2 guys hit the deck in a hurry. I got a blow on the old melon and that got me upset. Those guys learned that you do not mess with us. I had let out the distress whistle that we all knew and was real lucky that 2 of our sailors were within earshot and here they came. We had a good fight. One of the gooks tried some of his fancy judo but I had gotten my belt from a class that I had taken and that guy never stood a chance. He went over my shoulder and one of the sailors hit him with a roundhouse right before he even hit the deck. Another guy fell with my monkey fist in his chops. By that time there were only a couple of them standing and they begged for their health. End of fight and the sailors went back to work and I headed for the office.

My orders were to take a barge to Hawaii and bring back an empty. That barge was loaded with oil and was to be taken to the dock at Barbours Point. We were to tie up the loaded one and make up to the empty and head right back. OK, no problem.

Chapter 18

My boat was tied up at Pier 3 and so down the dock I went and got aboard. Most of the crew was there already. Three of the men were ones that had been with me before. Engineer, deckhand, mate were old hands but the cook was a new guy. The cook I liked had been sent to Alaska on another boat. The deckhand was an AB and he became the lead deckhand and proved to be a good one. I let them all know that we were to get underway as soon as everything was stowed and the engineer was ready.

We went over to the oil dock and made up to the barge. We had checked on the weather from here to Hawaii and the report was for good sailing so we put on one shot of chain. The chain was 75lbs per link and a shot was 90ft long. Lots of weight and held the tow line down so it did not fetch up and break.

One of the new guys was so anxious to please that actually he was in the way. He was trying to help and as Jack the lead deckhand was setting the shackle pin he got his hand in the way and ended up losing his index finger. "Balls" now we have to get him to a doctor and of course he was through for this trip. We wrapped his hand and gave him a pain pill and I had called for an ambulance to pick him up. Called the union hall and told them to send another man as soon as possible. The new guy showed up and he was someone that I knew from one of the trips to Alaska. The whole episode made us only about 2hrs late for our departure.

We had a good trip to Hawaii with no problems. The new man worked out real well and was able to do his share well. We tied up at Barbour's Point and made sure to get fuel etc. We also got some of that good Hawaiian food on board. Made up to the empty and headed for SF. Weather was fine with a little wind and chop off our port side but was good going so we could run at top rpms.

It was my watch and the lead deckhand was with me in the wheelhouse. He was steering and he said "what is that stuff off the starboard bow about ¼ mile ?". I slowed up to take a good look and they turned out to be Jap fishing floats. He said " it would sure be nice to have some of them."

It seemed to me that they would be a nice treat so I told him " to get some of the men and a boat hook etc and see if we can get some of them aboard." We played around with that for about an hour and got 30 of them. They were from 8inches to 2feet in diameter and some of them had the original netting still on them. What a find. Getting them off in SF might be a problem but we will figure that out when we get in. We stowed them in the lazarette for now. I still have two of them at home.

If a guy was lazy or did not know how to navigate all he had to do was to look up and run with the airplanes that go to and from Hawaii. One guy that I knew would shut the engine down and listen for them if it were overcast. He had done that for 16 years until the Coast Guard made everyone get a license and learn how to navigate. He laid off for 6months and went to school to learn so he could keep his job.

We got into SF at about 2400 hrs. I knew where to tie up the barge and then we went on over to pier 3 and tied up the boat. First thing was to get those floats off the boat. All the crew helped and we divided them up so that each guy would have his share.

I stayed aboard until the morning and went on in to the office and got my new orders.

Take off for a week and call in.

Chapter 19

It did not take me long to get that pickup started and off to home I went. It was about 1000hrs when I went across the bridge so the traffic was real light and it was a quick trip home. Gas was 25cents a gallon and we did not worry about having to fill up or how much it cost. We had a tank at the ranch and the gas company delivered for even less. The place looked real nice. No one was home so the big dog and I sat on the big swing set and waited. At last here they came the family and they were all surprised to see me and it was a bunch of hugging and kissing for sure. They were all in good shape and were all trying to talk at once. Always felt as though the wife and the kids really missed me, of course I surely did them. On the boat with the radios all barking at once and the radar going etc. it was easy to keep that organized but with all the kids and the wife all going at the same time it was hard for me to get it all. Oh well!

Oldest daughter wanted to become a vet and the second daughter a forester and the boy wanted to grow up.

Meal time was story telling time and sometimes things got real interesting. Always fun at the table.

Got a few things done but the week went by like a minute. Called the office and they said to call back in 4 days. They called me in 2 days and said to come in as there was to be a meeting the next day. So here I go again.

There were several people at the meeting that I knew and the first thing was to say hello and have a cup of coffee. At last the boss came in and told us all to sit down and he called the meeting to order.

"I want you to know that there have been some new developments and please pay attention. It will be necessary to learn and do some homework. After you have heard the news , please one at a time, let me know what you think about it. If you want to we can recess for a day so that you can study it some more. All the charts that you would be needing are here for you. As you already know the rest of the world depends on us and needs our help to show them what and how to do everything. In this case it is to deliver and install an oil drilling platform in Venezuela. There will be two barges, one the drill rig and the other pipe and tools etc that will be needed. Each one of your ideas will be listen to. Thank you for your attention and let us know your ideas."

It was something to think about for sure. The people in Venezuela were friendly enough and we would not have to fight our way in or out.

I had been into and through Panama several times so I could see no problem there. It looked like a straight run north of Venezuela and stay clear of the coast until abeam of Caracas and the charts read that there was plenty of water. Hell, I am ready to go if the company says to.

Anyhow all the wheels had their meetings and could not come up with a yea or nay. They called us back into another meeting only that there were only two men called in.

"What are your ideas and remarks? Bill we will hear from you first so Bob you go out and wait till we call you."

I went out and was wondering what in the hell is going on. After about 30 minutes I was called in to say my piece. Bill had gone out, everything was real secret.

"Your ideas,please." I said "ok here it is. It looks to me as though it would be a straight run to Panama and through to the other side. No problem from there to abeam of Caracas."

" it seems as though you are ready to do the job

but we know you. What else".

I told him that "I want a few members of my crew to be my choice, Harry as chief mate, John as cook and an engineer with experience, preferably Clay".

"We have a union for hiring a crew." " I replied that the union does not sail. I want those people if at all possible".

"We will think about it and please come back tomorrow at 0900."

Chapter 20

I went up the pier to the Greek restaurant. He was a friend and had a good menu and did not charge an arm and a leg.

A couple sailors that had been in one of the same boats that I had been in at some time or another were in there and of course we got to talking. They were both thinking about staying in the bay and work on the tour boats. They could be home most of the time that way. They said that the tour boats were hiring and as soon as they finished their meal they were going over and talk to them. Sure something to think about.

I got to the office at 0800 and of course the first thing was to get a cup of coffee. While I was sitting there several guys I knew came in and we said howdy. They were all working in different boats and all had berths. I waited and 0900 came around and I did not see Bill, guess he must have been held up in traffic.

Finally at 0930 I was told to come into the office.

"good morning and take a look at these charts and tell us what you think of them".

I could not see any problems with them and they were current charts. I said " that they look good to me but where are the rest of them?"

"You always come up with something, now what?"

"I want the charts that show the approaches and the harbor itself for Caracas."

"Good for you. Here they are and you have the job. Good sailing and lay out what you will need and the nearest time of departure. You will have the tug Ocean. She has just come from the yard and has had a complete survey. She is tied up here at pier 3 and your crew will be aboard in the morning."

"I will give you a report in two days. Thanks and now I need to use the telephone."

I called the wife and she was not real happy about my going on another voyage but she understood the routine and wished us a safe and fast trip.

I went to the boat and the engineer was already aboard and he was the one that I wanted. He had many years experience with all types of marine applications. He said that the engines are in perfect shape. Yep he said engines like in more than one.

Each was 3600 hp and of the newest design. Running with no tow it would be possible to get up to 14 knots easily. Of course the barges could not stand the pounding so it would be necessary to pay attention at all times to the sea. We would carry 120,000 gals of fuel but would have to look for fuel inside of 30 days. We could run longer but why not keep plenty of fuel on board. We could fuel in Panama and in Venezuela so we should not have to worry about that. We had one 21/4 inch tow line and one 3 inch line with about 2100 feet on each one.

The crew came aboard in the morning about 0800. They got their gear stowed and then had to get signed in. Each man had to have all of his current shots and an all waters merchant marine document. They all passed so now we had to get to work. All the men that I had asked for were on board.

One of the deckhands had more sea time than the others and also I had him on another boat and knew that he was a good sailor and knew his stuff. I put him on as lead deckhand and he would be in charge of the deck work.

I told him to check all the gear that was used on deck and also the towing equipment. He gave me a really good report. Some things needed to be replaced or repaired and all the pins, snotters, and tow lines needed grease. All the tie up lines were in order and there were extras in case they would be needed. This was a new boat and all these things had to be looked at while we were at the dock. It would be real hard to find lines etc. out at sea.

Harry the first mate, was of course doing his checking also and worked real well with the deckhands. John, the cook, was to get all the stores that he needs and make sure that there would be plenty as it may be hard to get any on the trip.

Clay, the engineer, was busy making sure that all the water, fuel, and oil were topped off and that all the engines ran well and that the generators were on line and did their jobs.

The second mate had his hands full making sure that all the charts were in order and up to date. He was young but did a good job and wanted to learn more about everything. Over all it looked as though we had a full crew and a well trained one.

"Chief, make sure that we have storm windows and if not tell the lead to get some made".

John got on the PA and "chow down, chow down". We all ate at the same time as it was not necessary to keep a watch. We had shrimp salad and the best chowder ever. I liked to eat with the whole crew as it was a time when they could talk and ask questions and tell stories.

I told them the story about grease. All the gear on the after deck had to be greased and made sure that each worked well. One time we had used a grease that contained graphite and it turned out that the vibration and the salt water caused the grease to solidify and froze things up real tight. Make sure that none of the grease that we are using contains graphite. We had to use sledge hammers in order to free up the pins that had become frozen in place.

All the crew got busy and went over everything and made reports back as soon as they found anything in question. We spent 2 days on this and then at last the boat was ready to go to sea.

Clay and I went over to pier 98 and looked the drill rig over. We checked the towing gear and made sure that it was in good shape because we were going to use it in towing the barge. It was loaded with 3inch tow line and looked as though it would do the job well.

A crew is to ride the drill rig all the way to Venezuela and so it was time for directions as to how the equipment works for towing. One of the men thought that it was a bunch of "bull shit" to have to listen to what I had to say. " If you don't want to listen and do as I say, you can get off now and I will hire someone that will listen." He shut up and learned to keep his mouth shut. I wanted the men to ask questions as this was real serious business. Out there on the ocean it could be too late to ask.

The use of the radio was one of things they were told about as we needed to communicate. In the case of emergency we could take fuel from the drill rig. The head man on the crew of the rig was familiar with most of the workings of a boat as well as the drill rig.

At last we were ready to sail. I called all the hands to a meeting and talked over every thing that we could think of. All of the men seemed to know what we were to do. OK we will leave the dock at 0600 and make up the tow.

Another tug had been assigned to assist in making up the tow. It took almost all day to get it all right and hooked up properly. It would be real hard to "fix" anything at sea.

The assist tug got the barge away from the dock and held it out in the stream. We worked the drill rig out into the stream and kept the towline up short. The assist tug held the barge until the crew could get the line run out but still kept the line up short.

The radio started a transmission, "tug ocean, tug ocean come in this is the barge". I replied " Ok barge what is it?"." We have slipped wire and are holding it short". "keep it on the short wire and I am going to come ahead and put some tension on".

"We will maintain this until we have cleared the bridge. Come back barge and talk to me".

The barge man came back and said "I understand and you are to let me know the next move".

Chapter 21

We headed for the bridge and since the tide was just starting to flood the barge did not wander and stayed right behind.

"Come in barge". "barge back". "Let me know when you are abeam the bridge piers".

It took almost a half hour for the tug and the drill rig to get through the bridge and then another 20 minutes or so to get the barge through.

"Tug Ocean come in". "I have you". "OK we are abeam now".

"Keep headway on the barge but start slipping wire. Run out 400 feet and hold it until I tell you to slip more. Make sure that you slip wire slowly."

The weather was almost perfect and we were able to continue out to the sea buoy without any trouble. Now is the time to get the rest of the wire slipped and steady her up.

The barge had about 2000 feet of wire out and was to maintain that for the tow. The drill rig was about 2000 feet behind the tug so the tow was about a mile long. Attach the small line and keep a 24 hour watch. Put up the snotters and pins and good sailing. It would be several months before we get back.

This crew is working out real well. The lead seaman sure knows his stuff and teaches the second and the ordinary well. Some guys that I have known "knew it all" and would not pass on anything. Too late to learn in case of emergency.

Weather was good with light airs and good visibility and the coffee arrived in the wheelhouse good and hot.

The drill rig wanted to yaw and get out of line but the barge acted like an anchor and held it so that it was not necessary to change RPM's. Looks like we will make 6 to 8 knots so long as the weather holds.

The weather report came in and they said that we would get 25 to 30 knot winds so we would have to watch out. It turned out that with the barge back there we had a good steadying platform that kept things in line but we did have to reduce RPM's. We were down to about 4 knots. It took us another 3 weeks to get down to Panama.

Going into Panama and the canal was going to be a real slow job. We had to shorten up the tow lines and we will need an assist tug to keep the barge in line. It came alongside the barge and when we went into the canal locks we did not have any room to spare. We made it through and then we had to wait in Gatun Lake until some ships got out of the way. At last we were told that we could enter the next locks. We went through with no extra room again and the assist tug stayed until we could get to the fuel dock and top off. Johnny loaded up with fresh fruit and lots of shrimp.

The open ocean sure looked good where we had some room. That canal chore was real tough. Here we go with the next stop Venezuela. The drill crew did real well streaming wire and also remembered to attach a small line onto the towline. Steered northeast by east and wanted to stay clear of the islands and shoal areas off Venezuela.

The weather was light-airs and nothing over 15knots all the way. Once in awhile we get smiled on and have good sailing. There were lots of schools of porpoises and each morning John would gather the shrimp and fish that had landed on the deck during the night. Many times there was enough for all hands at breakfast.

At last we were off Caracas and out about 30 miles. We had 2 radars, one 48mile and the other 24 mile range. Also in this new boat there was a depth finder so no longer did we need to use the lead line.

We worked our way into the waters off the coast and I had called for an assist tug. It seemed that the only tug they had was broken down so now this is going to be a problem getting into this harbor. Oh well!! I guess I should have not expected anything different. These backward countries are all alike with the manana attitude.

"Drill rig-drill rig come in ". "drill rig back" " guess what? There will be no assist tug. You will have to heave up wire and stand by. Wait until you hear from me". "yeh, ok".

We had heaved up the wire on the tug so we were running shorten up and were on the slow bell and going just fast enough to have some control. A small boat came alongside and a pilot came on board. Johnny spoke their lingo so we got along OK. The pilot knew the water and the conditions. We got into a real sheltered spot and were able to drop the tow line that ran from the drill rig to the barge.

Without the barge to worry about we put the drill rig in position for drilling. They put out their anchors and we let go from them and headed for the barge. We came alongside the barge and put her up to the dock and got her tied up. I thought that we were through but the drill rig wanted us to stand by. I was able to make contact with our office and they told me to stand-by as long as needed and until the rig released us. It turned out that we were there for over a month. We shifted the drill rig at least 10 times and each time we had to help them set their anchors. The water was between 100 and 200 feet deep so it was not a big problem.

The local people were typical of warm climate and were easy going but they sure kept us supplied with fresh fruit and vegetables and all kinds of meat and fish. The women made it clear that they liked the "gringos". Had to watch a couple of the guys to make sure that they did not wander too far. The girls came out in their boats and showed off their wares. Most of them were pretty and put on a real show.

We put into the fuel dock several times and each time tried to stay long enough for the men to go up town. The dock was in town so they did not have to go far.

One of the deckhands was a "ski". His last name was Stancheski and was really a nice guy but one of the gals in town got mad at him. She said that he did not pay her and owed her a dollar and caused a big loud problem. The cops grabbed him and into the local "hoosgow" he went. I had to go and rescue him. The girl said that he owed her a dollar and the cops wanted $5 for their trouble. Of course in order to save face I would not pay them until some haggling and hollering. It ended up costing $1.50 for the girl and $5.50 for the cops. Got my man back to the boat though. No sense giving him a lecture because he felt bad enough especially when he found out that the fines were deducted from his pay.

The crew on the drill rig were certainly well trained and did their jobs well. Non of the local people knew anything except "manana and no comprende". They did keep the fresh food coming though and that was great.

At last the rig had the drill pipe down and were drilling. The tug that was "broken down" all of a sudden was running and on the job. We had to spend about a week teaching them what to do. Of course most of the work was already done so they spent most of their time "standing by". Maybe we can at last head for home. A radio transmission came though from our office and we were relieved and could proceed for home. !WOW!

Went to the fuel dock and after a lot of "haggling" we got fuel. The guy at the fuel dock told us that we had been there only 3 days ago and that we should wait for a few more days to take on more fuel. I told him that we were leaving and we want to top off now. He would not listen and finally I had to get the police chief to come and talk to him. This took another day and was a big nuisance. At last he said OK and we took on almost 4000 gals. We had lost a day with the dummy. Oh! Well now we could head for home.

Chapter 22

It did not take us long to clear the sea buoy and get out into the open sea. Sure felt good to feel the boat come alive and start rolling and pitching.

We made our normal 0800 transmission to the office and were told to call back at 0900. I called them and it seems that there is a barge over at Galveston that needs to come back to SF and since we are running without a tow go over and get it. Well there goes any chance to be home for Christmas. "the life of a tugman".

Better check and see what there is for charts.

It turned out that we were out of charts for a direct run from here to there. There was one for the whole Gulf but no detail one. Oh well, make do with that.

We checked some of the old logs and set a course that would take us close to the Yucatan Channel.

I had a log book from another trip from Panama to Galveston so had to make do. We got our heads together and knew that if we could get over to the Yucatan Channel the rest would be easy. Went north west by west and it worked out well. Made the coast just south of the channel and then it was, around the peninsula and on our way to Galveston.

We tied up at our docks and asked about the barge. The dock master turned and pointed to a beat up older barge and said "there she is, just waiting for you". Guess that barge had been there a long time and had to be moved once in awhile when it got too much in their way. They were glad to be rid of it and all hands turned to. It took us a week to check it all over and made sure that she could make the trip. At last we had it all ready and got hooked up and away we went. It was now Dec. 15 so it would be one more Christmas out at sea.

The weather was about as good as ever and only had one real blow that kept us on the slow bell for almost 3 days. Pretty good for that time of year and soon Panama was in hailing distance. I got them on the radio and they said come on in and that they had lots of room. We went right on through and fueled up on the Pacific side and we were able to take on some stores. "Frisco here we come".

Once again we had good weather and calm seas all the way. Sure unusual for January. We got abeam of the sea buoy and called the office. They told us to come to Pier 3 and tie up.

All the logs and time sheets were turned in and they had the pay-off ready in two days. We had to wait for them to get all the "stuff" figured out and it really was a big job. So we were all happy that it took only 2 days. Each guy got his pay and stood by until all of us could leave in a group. Most of us had a car on the dock and we made sure that each man was safe before we split up and headed our separate ways.

I had been home for 2 days and a buddy called and he wanted to meet and talk about a job with Harbor Tours right there in the Bay. I had been thinking about having a job that would be close to home. The kids wanted me close and so did the wife. I have always liked sea duty but guess that now is the time to make a choice. Maybe I could try this new thing for a while.

The wife and I went on down to the "City" and looked around. We went down to the waterfront and got on one of the Tour Boats and took a ride around the bay. It was a narrated tour and actually was interesting and we both learned new things about the bay and the city. One of the deckhands had been on the whalers and had been working for years on the tours. He sure made it sound nice. He lived in the city and was home every night. Said that he made a good wage and had steady work.

We were next to fisherman's wharf so into one of the restaurants we go. We always talk about things and next to us was a guy that heard us talking about the tours and should we or should we not go to work there.

"hi Captain, what are you doing here"?

I turned and there was one of my men that had sailed with me. "Jerry, it is good to see you. How are you and what is new with you"?

"I am on the beach now and have been for about 3 years".

"What is the matter? Have you been sick or hurt"?

"No, I am working here on the boats".

I had to know more about this so I asked"what boats"?

" When I first came onto the beach I worked on day tug boats doing ship work or what ever. Then along came an old buddy of mine and he suggested that I look into a tour boat job. After looking that over I decided to try it out and as a result I have been with them steady. Going on two years now and it seems like I will stay. Even met a little {fair maiden} and we will be married soon. Yep can't beat it. Maybe you should look into it for yourself".

That just about settled it. First thing in the morning I am going to see about a job.

The next morning I headed for SF and found a long time parking place and went down to the docks. I spent several days just looking and checking out the possibilities. I found out that I would have to go to the union first and get signed up and pay all the fees etc. This was another union and had to start at the bottom. We could not bring our other union time or sea time along. Another five hundred up front and the dues had to be paid on time each month. So I had to think this over real well. I called the wife and told her to get on the bus and come on down to the city and help me to make this change. She showed up the next day and we got down to hashing it all out. One other thing is that all the time that I had at sea would not be carried over to this new union. What a racket.

There was a guy on the dock that I remembered from some trip out at sea and so I asked him about what he knew about these tours. He told me that they ran all the time and when a man is at last on steady with them he could expect to work year around. He also told me that if I were the least bit interested that I should be over there at the office first thing in the morning. Come to find out later, he had been sent out to get me in conversation and he could pass on the info.

Early the next morning I was at the office. The lady at the desk asked me what I needed and I told her that I was looking for a job. She gave me a big smile and asked me to wait for a minute. In about a minute the inner door opened and I was asked to enter. There at the desk was the same guy that had told me to come in the day before. He got up and offered his hand and said have a seat.

He said " I could have told you yesterday but there are a lot of guys that say they want a job but they don't follow up so I wanted to see if you would come in. You should know that if you want to be a Capt. On these passenger boats you have to go to the Coast Guard and find out what you have to do in order to get a license." Some how he had found out that I had run Tugboats.

I went to the Coast Guard and they gave me all the info in order to earn an endorsement. It was to be a written test and proved to be a really tough one.

While I was studying for that test I worked as a deckhand and went from one boat to another as I wanted to know each boat. There were 10 boats that I might be assigned to. One of the Captains and I seemed to hit it off real well and so I stayed on one of the boats that he would be running. He started in teaching me all that he could.

It was a real challenge being a deckhand because we had to be with the passengers all the time. Some of them were from other countries and they did not know our language so we had to take special care of them. I met a lot of them and visited with all that was possible. I have had invites from many of them to come and stay with them in their own countries.

Even the people that could not understand the narrations that were broadcast on the speakers still had fun just looking at the big bridges, buildings, and all the other sights. Sometimes the bay was full of ships and all kinds of small craft. There might be a tug boat working a ship or even a submarine on his way to Mare Island. Almost every day that had a little wind blowing there would be a race of sailboats, maybe 100 of them at one time.

One of the passengers asked me if it would be possible or permissible to go onto the streets and wander around? I told them that in America we may go almost anywhere that we want to. We can even go into most of the buildings. The police will not bother you. It was hard for some of those people to understand freedom.

One of the men asked me if I would take him and his family around and show them the City. I told him that a friend of mine does that for a living and I set up a trip for him. He came back 2 days later for another trip on the boats. He was very happy about the trip around the City. This time on the boat trip I asked him to come to the wheelhouse and ride with me.

Guess he was overwhelmed that he would be asked to be in the wheelhouse. He told his wife and kids to stay below and that he would be back soon.

I told the waiter at the concession stand to take care of the family and that I would pick up the tab. That little deal cost me over 20 dollars. Bet that he had a lot of stories to tell back in Italy

Chapter 23

At last I felt that I could pass that test and also I had the required time on a passenger vessel. That captain taught me well and had let me run the boats so I had a good chance to pass. I went to the Coast Guard and gave them my papers and they said OK sit over there. It seemed like it was hours before I was told to come into the exam room. Make out these papers and do not talk to anyone. Two or three other guys were in the room taking tests. The whole thing was very impersonal and strict. Guess I was supposed to be ill at ease but after tugs and running out at sea I sure was not going to let these sailors bother me. They did not but I was still careful. That test proved to be a tough one. The whole thing took 8hrs per day for 5 days. After I was done and turned in my papers after the second day the examiner told me to stand by while he looked it over. He leaned back in his chair and said that I would have to do better than this. Come back in one month if you want to try again. Each time that there was a screw up I had to wait a month before I could try again. It turned out that I came back four times and the fifth time I passed. The record for trying again went to a guy that I knew and he finally passed after 24 tries. The Coast Guard is really fussy when passengers are concerned and rightfully so. Finally I got my Captain license. I was working all the time as a deckhand and now that I can be a Captain I have to join another union. My time does not go with me and so it is starting over again.

This time the union charged me 1200 dollars for entry fee. This union was the Marine Engineers and the dues each month was 20$. Sure gets expensive.

The day came that I was assigned a boat. We had a lot of parties and good times celebrating my getting the license and now it was down to business.

I went to the office and got my daily report log and keys etc. and was told that my boat was not at the regular dock but over at another dock. The office clerk told me that I should be careful and not get lost. He did not give to me the key for the dock and I think that he wanted me to have to come back for the key after I had gotten down to the entrance to that dock. I asked about the key and he told me that it was not necessary. My crew was out in the waiting room and I told them to stand by and relax as we were not leaving. The smart ass office clerk said that "you had better get going or you will be late moving that boat". I said "No I am not going to walk all the way over there and have to come back for the dock key and even be later."

We were at a stand-off and about that time in walked the boss. "what's going on here?" I explained to him what had taken place and the sh-t hit the fan. "Go back to your paper shoveling union and get out of my hair. Capt. Bob, come with me."

I followed him into the main part of the office and he opened up a large door on one of the cabinets and started handing out keys to me. Each key was marked with a number and after handing out 15 keys he explained the system. He also gave to me a list of all the numbers and docks so that I could be able to tell which key went where. I had the keys to all the docks that we used. "Take care of these and make sure that only one man in your crew might use one if necessary. Do not make copies, if you need another one get one from the office. Sorry about this problem and on your first day too."

I thanked him and got my crew and headed for the dock. We were now in a hurry as my first run was to be in one hour.

The crew turned out to be a good one. They had the necessary jobs done so that we could sail in less time than usual. We had just cleared the dock and I had made my normal report to the Vessel Traffic Center and they told me that 10 Naval Vessels were coming into the Bay and to give them the right of way. Of course I replied yes sir.

They were a real sight and I had just loaded the passengers and got under way and the ships were all in view. My passengers got a real treat to see that many at one time.

Once in a while a movie star or other important person would be on board and I always tried to keep their identities quiet. Some of them had their body guards along but many would try to blend in and not even be noticed. One day a guy said "hey Cap do you have a minute?" "Yes what is it that you want?"

"I just wanted to tell you that I sure appreciate this trip and am enjoying it very much and also that you have not drawn attention to me."

I took a good look at him and realized that he was none other than Isaac Hays. There were many other times that 'big shots' were on board. My crew was told to keep their identities quiet. On one of the trips there was a woman on board that was not even a good American and when she asked me to let her come up to the wheel-house so that she could give a speech on the loud speaker system, I said "Lady if I had seen you at the boarding ramp I would have put a special watch on you and if you had caused any problem you would have been confined in the head until we got back to shore. No you may not speak and you may not come up to my wheel-house.

Have a good trip." I do not think that she had been told off before. If she had gone to the office and told the story to my boss she would have been told off a whole lot more forcefully than I had. He had seen a lot of action in the service and knew her from her un-American activities.

The radio came to life and started a transmission and I was told to come to the office as soon as possible. Now what? Can't think of any screw-ups but I could have done something. Maybe that woman deal, who knows? I was out on a run but at the end I would have about an hour lay over. As soon as we were tied up I got all my papers etc. gathered up and headed for the office.

One of my fellow skippers was coming down the ramp as I was going up and of course he had to let me know that he had heard the radio also. "Glad that it's you and not me". He could have said anything but that. I have had my license for only three months or so and sure am worried.

At the office I was greeted by one of the most pretty secretaries around. She said "please stand by and I will call the boss." She rang the number and the boss opened his door almost immediately and of course I thought OH OH.

He came right over and shook my hand and said'" Good to see you again. Come on in and have a seat. Coffee is ready if you want."

I have been [around the horn] and that pat on the back and the nicey- nicey stuff made me real uneasy. I was to find out that he is not one of those glad handers at all.

"We have been watching you and you seem to like people and get along well with kids."

"I try to do my job" I said.

"Cap' we have a tough one coming up in a few weeks and we want you to take the run. There is to be tour of 3 hours with 200 children on board. Any reason that you would not be able to handle that?"

" I will do my job and I can think of a few things that I will need and would appreciate if it can be taken care of."

He did not even bat an eye and said" ok let's have it and we will cooperate if it is possible."

Ok here goes. "I would like a three deck boat and 2 deckhands on each deck."

He looked at me for a long time. At least it seemed like a long time. His reply was" This is why we wanted you to do this tour. Your first thoughts are for safety and we sure do like that. Yes we will make sure that you have a three deck boat and two crew members on each deck."

" I must have 200 child life jackets. Coast Guard requires that each child have one. Please give me time to be on board with my crew ahead of time in order to stow them properly."

"You have the tour Captain was his reply."

"Just like that?" was my question.

He said" yes and good sailing."

I had 2 weeks to get ready for the kids and in the meantime I went ahead with the regular schedule.

Chapter 24

The next tour was one that had 400 passengers. There is a roaring ebb tide and it will be real rough at the Gate so will have to be very careful. Some of the skippers will not go under the bridge on an ebb tide. They would turn before they even got to the bridge and many people complained. One of the ads for the tours was that they would be able to go under the bridge and look up at the underside. Many people expect to do that and there were a lot of complaints. Not on my boat though because that skipper that was my teacher showed me how to do it safely. Some of the passengers asked a lot of questions, like " how did they hold up the deck until they got the supports up?' Stuff like that but there were always kids that were really interested in how and when. It occurred to me that maybe some of those kids would grow up and become engineers. Maybe some of those kids would go to the library and look up the bridge building. People were really interested and I think that it is a shame that more people can't see the wonders.

The Coast Guard came aboard one day when we were still at the dock and wanted to fill me in on all procedures dealing with the children. "Please wait until I can get the crew present to hear all of this." It took only a few minutes for the crew to assemble and the Coast Guard started in. They gave a good talk and then asked for questions. Joe asked to speak and his question was "Can I spank one of them if needed?" He was told no and just get to one of the teachers and have them take care of the problem. Anyhow I am sure that we can handle the youngsters well. The CG left and we were on our own.

We got everything ready and the day arrived to load and get underway on the BIG TRIP.

The crew and I got to the boat early and double- checked everything. All the lifejackets were in place and easy to get to in case we needed them in a hurry. The caterer had all the extra food and drinks etc. in order. The weather was just about perfect and it looked like everything is in order.

All the little darlings were on the dock, pushing and hollering as kids will do. I came out of the wheelhouse and using my loud speaker I got their attention. " Knock it off and quit that loud noise. If that is the way that you are going to act you can just stay on the dock. We will not put up with that foolishness on my boat. You could have heard a pin drop and even the sea gulls had shut up. Guess the kids got my message so we decided to load them.

There were 200 children and 100 chaperons and it looked as though the adults had heard my speech because they were watching the children well. They divided up the children and put them evenly on each deck and as the trip went along they changed decks so everyone had a chance to be "up top".

One of the kids told me that his Dad was in the Navy so that gave me an idea. "How about you being my first mate and that way you can keep these others in line." He jumped right onto that idea and went to do his job. I do not know how much he did but we sure did not have any trouble. Afterwards I thanked him and he gave me the smartest salute that I've seen.

I took them around Treasure Island and up the Oakland estuary and on over to Angel Island , out the Gate and around Alcatraz Island and all the time that we were on the go one of the men in the crew would be narrating. One of my men had a real gift of gab and he would tell lots of stories. The kids thought he was just great and each time that he would come out of the wheelhouse the kids would flock around him to hear more. Most of his stories were true with a little added flavor. I sure enjoyed having the kids.

This was a three hour trip and we had lots of time to show the youngsters the sights and also we were able to teach them history of the bay area. One of the teachers told me that she had learned enough to have many lectures about the area. This job was a whole lot different than the rough and tumble tug boating.

We got back to the dock and were tied up in good shape. The kids were all behaving and I am sure that they had learned a lot about the Bay Area and it's history. The lady that was in charge asked me to make sure that I would take out the next bunch of kids. She was going to see whether she could get these trips as a regular school function.

I liked tug boating but this tour business is growing on me.

The dock was my home while I was in the City. I got 2 days off each week but it got busier and I had less time off and some weeks I got no time off to go home. It sure was nice to have a good camper to stay in at the dock. I got lots of overtime and the pay was great. Every once in a while the wife would show up and stay for a week or so. Sure kept me honest and pure as it seemed that there were lots of women that wanted the Capt to keep them company. Some of the guys strayed and it was hard on their marriage and caused several of them to end up with divorces.

A lot of the men were so <rich> that they refused any overtime and that was fine with me as I worked all the overtime that I could. Sure looked nice on the paycheck. <infernal revenue> liked all the extra that they got too.

I had put in a couple weeks steady and so I decided to take a walk up the dock one evening and see what is happening at the neighborhood watering hole up at the end of the dock. I had a heave ahead and then another. There were a lot of sailors in the joint and I had lots of company. After awhile I thought I had better get on back to my camper so I started for the door and was stopped by a whole bunch of guys that worked on the same boats as I did. Nothing would do but to have a heave ahead with them. We "braced the yardarm" a few times and it was a good thing that I did not have to go back to work until 1300. That gave me time to get back to the camper and have a few hours sleep before having to go back to work.

Chapter 25

There is a place on the dock that is set aside for men to be able to rest, talk, read or just sit and listen to the ships radios. Ed and I were in there BSing and all of a sudden the radio came alive and one of the boats was in trouble. It seems that he had started to make the turn and enter the lane for docking and his engine had quit. Ed and I just got up and headed for the door. We went down to the dock where the water taxies tied up and there were two. One is a fast one and the other is a slower but husky work –horse. So we decided to take it and as I got the lines ready Ed started the engine and away we went. The boat we are after is not more than a block away so we were on her in a hurry. We came up from astern of her and slipped up real quiet.

We had our radio on so that we could listen in on any report. We made fast alongside and set up to take her in tow. Vessel Traffic center asked the disabled boat how it is going and the reply was the current seems to be taking us right into the dock.

We realized then that the skipper did not know that we were towing him in. The people in the boat were all dancing and the boat was going up and down with their music. They had all been having plenty of refreshments and having a good time dancing and they did not even know that we were alongside.

I said "Ed, this is going to be something, they do not even know what is happening".

"Yeh, let's keep quiet about all this and see what is going to happen."

We put the boat up to the dock and the deckhands made fast and we let go and just disappeared.

We started back to the water taxi dock and the radio started up again and it was Frank the skipper of the disabled boat. " vessel traffic center this is that disabled boat that I had reported an hour ago and we have drifted right up to the dock and are all tied up with no problems."

"You sure were lucky that the currents and wind were in your favor. Thank you for letting us know".

Ed and I busted up laughing and thought that this will be interesting as to how this will all turn out.

We went back to the ready room and the guys in there all wanted to tell us what had just happened. All we could say was " well isn't that something".

There were several reasons that no one including the skipper knew what was going on. First, it was a real dark night and the windows were all steamed up with all that dancing and coming up astern like we did was from the blind side so we got away with the whole caper without even being seen. Dam ain't we something? I was walking on the dock and Ed was coming towards me and when he got abeam of me I wanted to know if he was tied up. He started laughing and finally had to sit down he was going on so. Guess a guy could go on for years and not have something as good as this to take place again.

We went on down to the local sea food restaurant and we sat down and ordered coffee and fish and chips. In came Frank and I asked him to sit down and have some coffee. We were talking about the business when he says" let me tell you guys what happened to me and my boat last week".

"I had a whole boatload of passengers and we had just finished a charter and I had started to come in to the dock when the engine quit."

I said " boy that must have been a sinking feeling."

Ed looked real interested and asked " what did you do?"

Frank had an audience. This should be good.

"Yes it was sure something and of course I called Vessel Traffic Center to let them know that my boat is disabled and to warn other traffic. I did not want to tell the passengers for fear that they might panic and get out of control. I kept working the manual steering with the hope that it might help but for a long time there was no response and all of a sudden the current caught the boat and it started to move in the direction of the dock. You can not imagine the feeling that the boat was actually moving right to the dock. We got right in next to the dock and the deckhands made fast. I'll tell you that was really something, right to the dock. I called the center and told them about the current and that we were all secure."

Ed and I told him how lucky he was to go right to the dock like that. WOW! Just think, that boat could have gone almost anywhere but to go right to the dock. Man oh man that sure [was something.]

He had a real story to tell so Ed and I just kept quiet but commented how lucky he had been.

At the end of each month the boat hour meters were read and it was determined that one of the water taxi boats had 2 hours of unreported time. Neither Ed nor I told the office about the little caper. And Frank is telling how the current put him right up to the dock. We wonder what else we could do and get away with.

The time was coming up to bid on a new assignment. Every 3 months a man could bid on another boat or run and it was a good thing because it would give each guy a chance to change over to something new. I think that I will bid on the water taxi run and try that for a while.

I was at the ready room waiting for something to happen when in walked a guy that I had seen around the docks. He sat down just like he thought that he belonged here and started a conversation about boats etc. He talked like he knew about the docks, boats and other related things. Then he asked me what I did. Down here on the docks a smart person did not just volunteer any more information than necessary. I told him that I was in here just to rest and get off the street for a while. He said " yeah me too." I went back to my reading and after about 5 minutes he went back out the door. Guess he figured that I was not in the mood for talk or something. It was never a good thing to just volunteer info. Out here on the docks we did not even tell a stranger the "time of day."

About 2 weeks later came the time to bid on a new assignment and I had decided to bid on the boat that was docked 2 docks down from where the other boats were. It was a smaller boat and did not take as many passengers at a time. The steering was with a large 5ft wheel that was a challenge to operate. I figured that it would be fun to run and if I could get my regular crew I would enjoy the independence. The dock was not in the main tie up area and we would be on our own most of the time.

I submitted my bid and in a week the Company was to let us know the results. Guess I was the only one to bid on the "Gold Coast" because I got the job. Also I got my regular men. I was issued the keys etc. and told to go on over to the boat and make sure she would be ready to sail in two days.

We were checking her out from stem to stern and I had just closed the engine room hatch and discovered someone standing behind me. I knew that the crew was up on the second deck so I was prepared for what ever but not what I saw. Standing there was the same guy that had been in the ready room 2 weeks ago. I let him know that no people are allowed on the vessel and for him to leave. He said "he was sure glad to see me and let me introduce myself." " ok start talking." He did and I feel like a big jerk. He is the owner of the boat and had been trying to get a good crew. He said "you run the boat and here is my number to call if you need. Turn your logs into your office each day and good sailing."

Just like that and I'll tell you that I took a liking to him right now. Maybe this was a good thing that I had bid for this run.

All of these boats had a concession stand and served coffee, sandwiches etc. and so far I had not heard anything from that dept. The office for the stands was only about a block away so I walked over there and asked them if they were told that the Gold Coast boat was back and needed stocking and that we will need an attendant. "Nobody told us anything about it but we will get right on it." Sure am glad that I had gone on down to the office. One of the gals that takes care of the stands was in the office right then and asked me if she could have the job. I knew the gal from some of the other boats and said that she sure could if that is OK with everyone. Not only is she great in her job she is also a good looker and real pleasing. Would be an asset for our boat. I told her to come on down and look it over and that we have another week before we sail. I did not want to lose her so I said "your pay time starts in the morning." There was lots to do to get her station ready for customers. I am happy about getting her but hope the wife feels the same way. I do not know what I was worrying about because I found out about 3 weeks later that they had known each other and got along well.

We had checked over all the running gear and I had checked the wheelhouse gear. The engine indicators, radar, lights, radios and all the other gear worked well so let's go.

Chapter 26

We were to take on a special tour for the first run. The group is the High School Glee Club from Walnut Creek. They turned out to be a really nice bunch of kids. Half way through the tour they want to sing so I told them to get with it. They had some instruments and could sure sing. I think that they can be heard all the way up town. This is a fun time for sure. The club director wanted to ride with me in the wheelhouse. She is full of questions about the area so I sent word to have Jim come up to the wheelhouse. He is a really good narrator and knew all the right answers. It turned out to be a real success. This is a 21/2 hour tour and the next one is already on the dock. Looks to me that this tour boat is going to be real popular.

The next tour was a regular one that went under the Golden Gate Bridge. My head narrator was in his element as he could put more interesting facts in his narration than anyone else. In fact he taught me a lot of things about the area. He had been around a long time in the bay area. He and his family had been evacuated from SF to Tiburon after the big earthquake in 1906.

Coming back to the dock from out in the bay I have to slow down and not cause wake problems to the boats that are tied up along the docks.

One of the boat's skipper has the loudest voice that I have ever heard and he likes to use it. Almost each time that I come along he bellows out and says something.

We sure have a good bunch of people on the boat and everyone is enjoying themselves and they are busy gathering up kids and personal gear because we are almost up to our dock.

That loud mouth hollers out "slow down you SOB, you are making a huge wake and are damaging my boat." I am on the slow bell and barely moving so he is just being a jerk. So I just waved at him and did not even leave the famous finger sticking up.

We got unloaded and I made out my logs and now I have to check the engines as we are to leave again in about an hour. I am closing up the hatch at the engine room and felt someone behind me. I turned and there was that jerk, on my boat.

The tension has been building for weeks and it is hard on me because some of the passengers have said things about him and they do not need any bad vibes. Only one thing to do now that he is on my boat and it looks like he wants trouble. He got his mouth in gear and I knew that we were going to fight. It says in the rule book that there will be no fighting aboard a boat. It is a clause on page 16 and is very emphatic about the fact. OK, I have to get him off the boat.

I began backing up and he came right after me and at last I got him over on the ramp and off the boat. Now you big ass you are to learn a lesson about calling me a SOB. This is still company property but nothing is in the book about fighting on the ramp.

His mouth is in gear again and before he can get over loud I tapped him to get him to shut up. I sure do not want a crowd to form. He is just about to make a big mistake. He hit me a blow and now I am mad. I hit him and spun him around so that now he is backing up the ramp. I hit him each step and since the ramp is 30 feet long I got him good all the way up and through the gate at the top. Herb had gone up and had the gate open for his departure. I hit him a full right to the gut and an upper cut that finished him off. Herb and I went on back down to the boat. We did not have to load for another 45 minutes and Herb checked to make sure that a passed out piece of crap was not in the way. Bet he will not be hollering at me anymore and he will not go on another boat without permission.

We do not have to load for another 30 minutes but my hands are starting to swell. Paula at the concession stand got me some ice in cold water and told me to put them in and be quiet. As soon as my hands were in that water they sure hurt. About 5 min. later they began to feel better so now at least I can grab the wheel and steer the boat.

We are loading and in the crowd is my buddy from the office. Of course I am expecting a lot of flap about the fight but hope not. We finished loading and got things secure. Ok, throw off the lines and we will get underway. There are only 105 passengers on this trip and so the people will have lots of room to move around. Bob from the office has not come up to the wheel house yet and now I am wondering. Jim is narrating and Herb is on the main deck circulating and I see Bob talking to some people on the second deck. He is pointing and telling the passengers by him a story I guess. Anyhow he is acting as though he does not even want to see me, which is fine with me. My hands are pretty swelled up and I have a bruise on my cheek where that guy tapped me and I feel like I can't hide what had happened in the fight. I know dad gummed well that he must have heard about it otherwise how come he is on my boat right now. The radio is barking and vessel traffic center is advising all boats, of traffic at the bridge both outgoing and in coming so I have to pay attention to my business and not worry about him.

The traffic was not that bad at the Gate and we went on through and made the turn fine and headed back to the dock. He still has not come to the wheelhouse. We got tied up and the passengers are unloading and I am watching from the stanchion on the second deck. They are moving along fine and Herb and Jim are helping but still no Bob. There he is at last moving out onto the ramp. He turns and hollers up to me "see you later, good run".

He is walking slowly up the ramp and seems to be looking at the deck as he is going. He is really looking as he is going through the gate at the top and finally gets to the place where there is a little blood from that fight. He turns and looks right at me and gives me a , big thumbs up. He knows all right. Never heard anything more about it.

Chapter 27

I think that it is about time that I just go on down to pier 39 and up to the Café and BS for a while.

" Hi Danny, what's new on the waterfront?"

" Same old 6's and 8's Capt. How's the wife?"

"Doing fine Danny and she is real happy about this job. I can get home almost every week."

Danny is a real good man and takes care of the people that are in his place unless they get out of hand. "Do want a drink or you just want to talk?'

"Yeah, I could sure use one. Same thing as usual."

He was making my drink and I told him that I had tomorrow off and I noticed that he put an extra amount of vodka in. I have seen him cut down on a guy's drink if he were getting too much.

"She will be down for a few days and should be coming in at any time."

He told me "You sure had better bring her in to see us because my wife and I think that she is the best."

"Oh, she'll be in but I have no idea just when she will arrive. She can't leave the place up north any ol'time that she wants."

"Does she still have horses, cows, and all the rest of the farm animals?" he asked.

"Yes she does and the kids are in all kinds of things with the school. They are a big help around the place and do the heavy stuff. She gave up the tractor work and the roto tilling."

Each day there are the regular bunch of sailors, city workers, cops, and others, that make the place a colorful place to be. In the morning comes the breakfast crowd and at noon comes the lunch bunch and as the wife says," next comes the others."

Danny was mixing another for me when in came Bernie.

"Where the hell have you been Bernie haven't seen you in a long time" was my greeting. "have one on me?"

" About time you bought one, and what have you been doing for excitement?"

I said "nothing much just work and more work and no time for play."

Bernie is an ok guy but does not use his head sometimes and replied to me " yeah sure we know."

I asked" what do you mean, yeah sure?"

He grinned and looked serious and said " you know what I mean."

I finished my drink and went out the door. Never did like that [you know what I mean stuff}.

Went over to Chic's place. It is a restaurant and bar and I've known him for a long time. I sailed with him a long time ago on board a tugboat.

I went up to the bar and ordered a drink. The bartender could sure make a drink, 95% vodka and a smidgen of 7up.

Thor, Chuck and Hank came in and of course we took turns buying. Dammed good thing that I have tomorrow off. We chewed the fat and sailed all over and always told the truth. We must have been in most of the boats in the world. I have always enjoyed listening and sometimes I learn a few things.

We had another round and Chuck said," let's go over to the Eagle and see what's happening."

The distance to the Eagle from Chic's is not very far but with our wanderings it was a lot further. At last we arrived and when we entered we found the place full and standing room only. "Look up the bar and see that pretty gal" Thor said. I did and there is my wife talking to Danny.

I had no idea how long she had been there so I looked at my watch and we had been at Chic's for a couple hours. Danny came down the bar and told me that she has been here for 10 min. or so. Dammed good thing that I had not stayed over at the other place longer.

Might as well go over to her and say hello. I have no idea if she is mad or not. I put my hand on her shoulder and she turned and saw me and planted the nicest kiss ever. She is not mad and seems to be happy to see me.

Danny always takes care of the wives that belong to us sailors. Sometimes wives will show up 2 or 3 hours before a guy gets off work and he makes sure that they are safe.

The city had passed a law so we could not even dance. Too bad, so we ordered another go around and sat back to pass the time together.

After another one we headed for the camper. "I will get you to the camper and then go and get your bags from the car." I was trying to be nice.

She said," that won't be necessary to get my bags because they are in the camper already."

" When did you get to the city?" I asked.

" About 3 this after noon and first I took a nap and then went shopping and came back to the camper and still no you so I went to the Eagle because I knew that sooner or later you would end up here and I wanted to visit with Danny anyhow."

" I'm hungry so let's go get something."

Chapter 28

We went over to the Chinese place and had a good supper and by that

time it was late so time to get some sleep. Morning came early and it was back to work for me. She stayed in the sack and would join me later on the boat.

I had stopped in at the office and was told that we were to have a Coast Guard inspection at 0800.

That did not leave me much time as it was already 0630. The crew would be on board at 0700 so I had better get going and open the boat. As soon as the men get here we have a lot to do.

" Good morning you lucky people, we are to have a Coast Guard inspection at 0800. It is sure nice of them to tell us so early!"

Our first run is at 1100 and they will be here at any time. Sure hope they don't take long because all the jackets etc have to be stowed before we can load.

Jim and Herb turned to and knew about breaking out all the gear to be inspected. Two guys walked onto the boat and said that they are to help with the gear etc. What a relief, now we can get it all done in time.

I had to get all the wheelhouse gear ready. Radar, radios, compass and even have to show that the wind shield wipers are in good shape.

The Coast Guard is always on the ball and I don't mind them having the inspections. If they didn't the boats might get sloppy and if an emergency did happen somebody could be hurt.

The inspection went well and with those two extra guys we were ready to load on time. I am real glad to have Jim and Herb to sail with.

Jim is full of knowledge and is telling a great story about the 1906 earthquake and all of a sudden he said " Man overboard- man overboard!" He went into action and I took over the PA system.

" Passengers pay attention- stay away from the sides and give my men all the room that you can. Do not try to help. They are trained and know their job! "

" This is to be a starboard side pick-up. I have him in sight and will get close."

He seems to be weakening and there he goes under. Herb had on a jacket with a line attached and in the drink he went. He got a hand hold on that guy and Jim started pulling them in. I have to get down to the main deck and give him a hand but I looked up and there is the Coast Guard boat. They came right in and picked up that guy and then got Herb back on board. Two of the crew on the Coast Guard boat were at the inspection this morning. They sure do a great job.

A woman was on the second deck crying and carrying on and looked as though she needs help. I asked her if she knows that man and she said " yes he is my husband."

We were about 1 mile from the dock." Vessel Traffic Center this is the Gold Coast and we have completed the rescue of the man overboard and we are going back to the dock as we need a doctor and ambulance."

" Gold Coast this is the office and we will have the doctor and ambulance waiting at the dock."

"Thanks, and we want to continue with the tour if that is OK with you."

" OK with us- office clear."

"Jim give these people a little talk and if they want to continue the tour, we will."

The woman is real happy that we had made the arrangements and as soon as she is off the boat, away we go.

The passengers are a good bunch of people and will have tales to tell at home.

We have another tour after dark. It is clear and will be dark with no moon so the lights from the city will show up.

We are back at the dock. Now we will get ready for the night trip. There will be sandwiches and coffee and the bar will be open. We won't leave for 2 hours. It is clear weather and there is no moon so the bright lights of the city will show up real well.

Chapter 29

We were just sitting around the next day, passing the time and Herb asked, "Are you going to bid the Gold Coast again?"

"I haven't given it much thought but guess that it is that time. What is your choice?"

"Well I want to stay on your crew Capt and since I have enough seniority I can bid anything I want. Let me know when you have made a decision and I will bid with you."

That gave me something to ponder but he is a good sailor and is real good with people and I like him anyhow.

I think it is about that time to say hello at the Eagle so here goes.

I said howdy all around and ordered a drink. I happened to sit next to a man who is a race car driver and also is a Capt with the other company. He has a nickname of final-final.

Jim came in and came right up to me and said

"Have you bid yet?"

"No, not yet. Have you?"

Capt, tell me as soon as you do because I want to be on your crew.

What the hell can I do but to bid the Gold Coast? Those are two great guys, good sailors and they enjoy their jobs.

In came my concession stand gal and she sat next to me so I asked if she wanted a heave ahead? She did and before another minute went by, she asked me about the bid. It began to look like they had all gotten together on this bid thing. She said "if you are going to stay on the Gold Coast then I want to be there too."

Yep seems like I don't have any choice so "yes I will bid the Gold Coast."

"Good, I like that run too." She said with that great big smile.

Here comes my buddy Tom [her husband].

"All day you are with my wife and now you are with her at the bar."

"So what, she is a wonderful lady and deserves a good job and anyhow I'm buying."

"It's time you did. I will have one too."

So it is going to be a fun evening.

Her husband is a commercial fisherman and is a good man to talk to. The government is making it harder and more expensive to make a living. He has almost a daily run in with one official or another.

Final-final was on his 3ʳᵈ or 4ᵗʰ and I was going to buy him a drink but thought I would ask him first.

" How about another drink, my friend?"

"Ok but this is the final-final."

We had a good evening with not even one argument or fight. There was a lot of talk and opinions about port and starboard and who has the right of way, but that is normal.

In the morning I have to put in my bid for the Gold Coast. Most of the skippers don't like running the boat because of the shifting and steering. I like it because it sure keeps me in good shape and is no problem for me. I can take it for the next 3 months and then the rules say that I will have to bid for some other run. They say no more than 6 months in a row on any run.

Day after tomorrow we have to take the boat over to the maintenance dock and have the oil changed and engines checked over. We will also take on fuel while there.

I told the men to bring an overnight bag because it might be that we will be staying over. "If we do stay over your pay keeps right on running and you get a bonus also."

That part of town where we had to go is not a good place. Too dam many dopers and punks. I put my 38 pistol in my bag and I made sure that my boot knife is sharp.

We got to the dock ok but on the way in there are several loafers and punks watching. Jim came up to the wheelhouse and asked if I had seen them.

"I saw them for sure and now we will have to be on watch all night. You take the first watch, Herb the second and I will take the last."

Last year an engineer friend was in a boat that was tied up at Pt. Richmond. All of the crew had gone into town and he stayed on board because he had some special work to do on the equipment. He was found dead. The boat had been ransacked and he had been robbed. As far as I know there has never been an arrest.

My crew and I do not intend to be another statistic. There is movement out on the dock behind the screen. I figured that it will take a while for those punks to build up their courage. We could see them drinking and smoking pot and taking whatever else they can find.

It is now about 0130 and is about the right time for them to start something. I got Jim and Herb up and told them to get ready.

Sure enough here they come. They had a small aluminum boat and loaded with too many for the size of it. We stayed out of sight and guess they thought that we were asleep or gone. They got real close and within good easy shooting range and I let go with several shots and put holes in their boat. They are screaming and making a lot of noise and the boat is taking on water. Herb said " look up there" and pointed to the end of the dock. The cops are here and they will fix those punks. The punks are rowing for all they are worth and are heading right for the cops. I'll bet those guys can't swim because they could maybe get away if they swam under the dock and kept quiet. HA-HA

The cops got all of them and called in another car to haul them away. The boat sank.

We did not hear anything more about that, but we also did not see those punks again.

All we have t do now is to fuel up and we can get back to work.

Chapter 30

The bids have gone through so we are back to the same crew and it sure is nice.

We are to work today and then we have 2 whole days off.

The office just called and asked if we could be ready to take a bunch up to the moth ball fleet and show it to them and tell them the story. Jim is well trained in all the ship movements and anchoring in the fleet area. I think that he could go on for hours about the world war two ships and others that are there. I asked them how soon and was told in about an hour. Ok we are ready.

It turned out that they are a bunch of history majors and most of them are from the bay area. Jim was sure busy telling them the stories of the ships and Herb was busy telling them what he knew. The teacher is a good looking, interesting young lady and wants to stay with me in the wheelhouse. No place to sit down but guess that she doesn't mind. She is from Idaho and has never been on boats before.

"Do you live in San Francisco?' she asked

"Oh yeah it's ok."

Her next question was something "What do you do after hours?"

"Oh, we go to the Eagle Café and have a few. Mostly sailors hang out there."

"Maybe I'll see you there. Do they have food?"

"No, not after noon."

This run took us past Angel Island and Richmond. Then under the Richmond Bridge, through the Straits and under the bridge that separates Pinole and Vallejo and then on to Martinez and under that bridge and on to the fleet. It is a long run with lots to look at on the way.

They all had a good time and I am sure learned a lot about the area. It became a regular tour and was a good education for the students. Also it was a good money maker for the company.

A few nights later I was at the Eagle and in walked that teacher. She came right over and sat next to me. " The students and I surely enjoyed the trip and hope to do it again."

"You should go over to the office and set up a regular run for each month." I told her and hoped that she would.

" One thing for sure is that you would have to run the boat."

"I'll do what I can but can't guaranty that I will still be on that run."

The door to the café opened and in walked my wife. She came right up to me and planted a great big kiss and said hello.

The teacher said "Well, guess I should have kissed you!"

I replied with "She married me first."

"Rosie meet my wife Nan."

This was getting kind of strained and right then in walked Joe. I have known him for some time and at one time had been my deckhand.

" Hey Joe, sure good to see you, remember my wife Nan?"

"Hello again, it has been a long time, I just got in from Alaska."

"We want you to meet our friend Rosie, Joe."

Rosie perked right up and asked "Have you known Capt long?"

Joe said," Oh, a couple years or so."

And that was all it took. They started talking like they had known each other for a long time. In fact they got up and moved over to a table and took their drinks with them and sat down and got cozy. Sure hope that she goes ahead and sets up more trips with the kids.

Nan looked at me but didn't say a word.

" It is getting late and I have a 0900 run in the morning so let's go and get some chow and hit the sack early."

I got to the boat early at 0730 and a few minutes later Paula came on board. "Coffee will be ready real soon."

It was ready by 0800 and Herb and Jim had some and I asked Paula if she was ready to load and Jim was ready so we started loading. We were not to leave until 0900 and the people that came on went right to see Paula and got coffee. We made enough off the coffee to pay the fuel bill for all day.

The group was a mixed bunch with some children.

"Traffic Center this is the Gold Coast departing the dock on a routine cruise."

"Traffic center back to the Gold Coast. Be advised that the carrier Midway is in bound and will be in the normal traffic pattern."

"Gold Coast back- we acknowledge and will take appropriate action. Thank you Gold Coast clear."

Jim had a lot of info .and was right in his element.

The carrier was just coming up to the bridge and I had slowed up to let her come on through before I got under the bridge also.

" Carrier Midway come in this is the Gold Coast."

" Midway back and what is your pleasure?"

" Gold Coast back- tell Captain Hollingsworth that I will pass on your port side. Gold Coast clear."

" Midway back to the Gold Coast- the will be fine Capt. Bob and it is good to be home."

Jim came into the wheelhouse and asked if he had heard that message right. I let him know that that Captain is a neighbor of mine and that my kids use his swimming pool all the time and he and I prune the vineyard together.

There must be 1000 people on the bridge watching the carrier.

Here we go again. One of the passengers wanted to know how we are going to turn around and what are we doing out here now that it is so rough?

"Guess we will play it by ear-just hang on."

I made the turn and was almost back to the bridge and here she came.

"When did you make the turn and how come we are back under the bridge again?"

Nothing for me to say so I merely pointed out something up ahead. This job gets to a lot of the guys. Usually the problem is the absolute ignorance

Of some people.

"Lady do you have any children with you?"

"No I am by myself."

"OK you are to stay in the wheelhouse with me and do as I say."

"Coast Guard station at Fort Point-come in"

" This is the Coast Guard at Fort Point"

"This is the Gold Coast and I am under the bridge now and off to the port side is a body in the water."

"Coast Guard back-we are underway and will be there in a few minutes.

"Gold Coast back-I will stay here and as you get close I will show you the body."

"Lady get back over there and stay put."

"Capt go over there and get closer!"

"If I were to get over there every person on this boat would run to one side and we would have a real dangerous list."

Most of the people do not even know what is happening. They think that we are showing them the bridge. Jim was talking about that and they were busy looking at it. Whew!

"Gold Coast we are almost up to you."

"Ok, hold your course and I will direct you."

"The body is approximately 2 points on your starboard bow at about 500ft."

"Gold Coast- we have it in view. You may leave the area now if you wish."

"Ok we are leaving and thank you for the quick response."

"Lady, you have just witnessed a terrible thing and something that happens too often. Please I am feeling foolish calling you Lady, you must have a name."

"Yes I'm Mary Williams. Here is my card."

"Wow, you are with the Sacramento Bee newspaper."

"Now that you know I'm with the paper I want you to know that I will write a story about this trip and we will send you a copy."

"Sure hope that you are nice with your reporting and it would be great to have a copy."

The rest of the trip was routine and after we were unloaded and the crew cleaned up we went to the local restaurant for lunch. Even Paula joined us and the reporter was at the table next to us.

We have two runs each day for the next 2 days and then we are to have another one of those long runs with the kids. I have to get more life jackets for that run.

Chapter 31

This job is real interesting but once again it will be bid time. I have to change runs this time around.

"You guys had better start to plan about what we are to do on the new run." I brought it up because I would like to keep my same crew.

Both Jim and Herb have mentioned the Angel Island to Berkeley run and I think that it would be a good one. We would have to have another crew member for that run. The boat for that run is bigger and holds more people.

We all showed up for the bid and got it. I do not know who the new guy is to be but we will worry about that later.

We got the boat's equipment ready and checked over and a concession guy came on board and loaded up. Looks like we are ready so "Single up the lines and let's go." The spring line was still fast and had not been taken off and I looked up and down the ramp on the run came Paula. She jumped on board and the guy that had loaded up the concession stand jumped off. I have my old crew back!!

When she had a chance she came up to the wheelhouse and told me the story. It went something like this.

"I wanted this run all along but for some reason the boss sent George instead. I found out in time and told the boss that if he was not going to let me have this run I'll quit. He told me right off that if I could get to the boat before it sails I could have the job. As it was I dam near did not make it."

Hell, I would have come back for her but I didn't tell her so.

Herb came up and told me that it is real easy to get stuck in the mud alongside the Berkeley pier.

" I was in that boat several years ago that had gotten stuck so bad that we had to wait until high water to get going again. Best thing is to stay about 400 ft. off the pier and run parallel to it and always run in the same trench each day.

That is one reason that I feel as though we are the best crew on the bay. I learned to keep in the trench day after day each time I ran that run. After several trips it was easier going and was sure easy to tell if I was in the trench or not.

We ran into another thing along that pier and that is that a few of the fishermen on the dock try to cast all the way over to the boat. I talked to the local cops about that but I might as well talk to the bulkhead for all they cared. If one of those sinkers were to hit someone on the boat it would cause a serious injury or worse.

We got to the dock at Berkeley and were tied up and still had 30 minutes before we were to load. Even with slowing down we still had plenty of time to keep to the schedule.

If I were to speed up, the stern of the boat would be sucked down and slow us even more. We loaded 200 people and so now I will have to be careful because of the extra weight.

You would think that some of those people are going to spend days on the island. One of the families even had a tent. " You know that you are not allowed to stay overnight on the island."

He answered, "I have never been on an island before and I want to be prepared."

Some of them have BBQs. After a few trips these people will know what to bring.

"Put out the bow lines and the stern line as well as the spring because of the current that might be running here at the island."

No one is allowed to stay overnight and it is up to us to pick up the same numbers of people as we had brought over. Another of our boats brings over and picks up people also so how can we be sure of the numbers? I got no answer at the office. It looks to me that it is up to the Park employees to keep track of the numbers.

"Make sure when you are loading that this boat is allowed to carry no more than 400 including crew so count carefully."

After we had gotten unloaded we were to go to SF with an empty boat. I'll bet that it won't be long before people figure out that they could stay on board and go to SF, shop or whatever and get on the boat again after the bay cruise. They could stay on and then go on to Berkeley. It would be a nice way to spend the day, for sure.

We got loaded and headed for Berkeley and it seemed that everything had gone well. I had no idea of any problems. Most boat people are a good bunch but there are some that look for trouble.

Jim had said "Look at those people on that boat waving and looks like hollering. They look like they are pissed about something."

On the way to Berkeley I received a radio message that told me to report to the office as soon as possible after we get back to SF.

Went into the office and there was the boss, even though it was after his hours.

"You sure are getting popular with the Coast Guard because you are to report to them at 0800 tomorrow. We have called in a replacement to take over this run until the matter is settled."

"Do you have any idea what the problem is ?"

"It seems that you are being accused of causing damage to one of the boats that is anchored at Angel Island."

"Let me see the papers." He gave to me a very important looking document. I read the paper and told him that "I have never ever read so much bull-shit in all my life."

In the morning I got me a cab and headed for the Coast Guard. The cab driver told me that he sure has a lot of business taking guys there.

In the office was my buddy the Chief. "Good morning Chief what now?"

"You tell me what now!"

"First place, it is impossible to make a wake big enough to cause any boat a problem there. Do me a favor and come aboard the my boat and I will show you."

"OK, I'll do that for you. This whole thing is serious and could cause you a suspension or even the loss of your license. Call me when you can set up the time and I will come out in one of our boats."

We set up a time and he came right over to Angel Island and met with me. After telling me what to do he sat back and just watched. First I went on the slow bell, explaining that is the usual speed that I use. Next I hooked it on and went too damned fast but I proved to him that it was impossible to build up a wake in that short run to cause anyone damage. That jerk that had made the trouble was watching.

Chief said," Well that settles it. In my report I will tell about this and you should not have any more problems. Sure wish people would not be so quick to cause trouble. Nice to see you Capt and I am going to bring my family and go on a trip with you."

"OK men, single up and let's go to the trench. There are 358 people on board so guess the company can make some money."

I have to go up to Napa to meet a buddy and be at a Rotary dinner tomorrow. That should be fun and will be nice to do something different.

We walked in and Bill sure knew a lot of the people. The speeches etc. are the usual but wish they would get done talking cause I'm hungry.

Finally we all got served and sure looked good. Everyone was doing the best to out talk the other guy. Across from me is a guy that is talking about boats and so of course I am listening.

It seems that the guy anchors at Angel Island and enjoys the area and spends weekends there. He started talking about "those" big boats that come and go at the island. " They come in and make a lot of noise and a big wake. One of them came in and made such a big wake that it caused damage to my boat. I turned that boat in and ended up with a new paint job."

" Wow, that boat must have caused you a lot of problems!"

"Not really but the company paid off like clock work. In fact I could have done nothing but I wanted a new color for my boat."

Well that was all that I was going to listen to so in no uncertain terms I told him "that he had pulled my chain long enough."

" You damned cheat and no good bastard I am the Captain of that boat that you said caused you so much damage!" I hoped that he would come over the table but like most of that type he just sat there.

"You saw the Coast Guard on my boat the other day and I proved to them that it was impossible to make a wake to cause you trouble. You could have cost me my license and now that I have found out that you are a big car dealer you will be hearing from me." He sure lost a lot of business after that.

We ran that run for another month and a half and I never saw that small boat at Angel Island again.

" I hate to say this but it is once again "bid time".

" I am going to bid this run again. We have the trench open and we have a good system. One more three months will put us into winter and this run closes down anyhow. Hope you guys will bid with me."

"You did not say anything about me and I would like to stay on this run."

I turned and there stood Paula. I said " Thanks Paula we need you."

Well I have my same crew and am set up until winter. Sure is a popular run and I am glad that there is a place around that those city people can go to and find out what it feels like to get off pavement and concrete.

Chapter 32

Winter came and I am not in a hurry to jump into another run right away.

I was just walking around the water front looking at all the activity when the boss came up to me and said that he was going over to Frank's for lunch and that he will buy. Fine with me so here we are.

The waiter came and I asked for the dinner menu. I noticed that the boss kind of shifted in his seat and I asked if he knew whether the steaks were good. Now I had him really worried.

The waiter came back and asked if we had made a decision and I said," yes I will have a bowl of your soup of the day and some bread."

"Whew, you had me worried because I have only 10 dollars and I sure as hell did not want to write a check."

" Well you said you would buy and I just wanted to pull your leg."

It was real good soup but I realized that he had more on his mind than my stomach.

We settled back with a cup of coffee and at last he got to the point.

"I want you to bid the water taxies. We have a lot of trouble now on that run and we want you to straighten out the problems."

First time I had heard about problems so I asked him "What problems."

He said, " Drunken crews from the ships, fights on board and the boats are getting lost and have a hard time in finding the ships."

" I know that sometimes there can be many ships out at the anchorage waiting for dock space etc. but are the water taxies equipped with radar?"

The boss said, " Some of them but even the boats with radar get lost. There are no big signs on the ships that say here I am."

" Hell, sounds like fun and I will bid for them."

It seems like most of the troubles come late at night so I bib the 2000 to 0400 watch. I got that watch ok and went to work.

I am at the water taxi's dispatch office and there are 6 people waiting for the boat. Guess I had better get busy.

I went down to the boat and checked over the engines and pumps etc. They are in good shape and in the wheelhouse I got the radar running and set and started up the engines. Tossed off the lines and went over to the loading dock. Now there are the 6 from the office plus another 10 that had been dropped off by taxi-cab. There are two women in the bunch. I had learned a long time ago to pay attention to the presence of women because a lot of the problems have been because of them. The problems were not the women but some drunken sailor that is trying to put on a hit.

I went out to throw off the line and while I was out on the dock two of the guys off the Norwegian ship had gotten into the wheelhouse and the decided that they were going to run the boat. I was able to convince them to go back down into the seating area and stay there. Another sailor started up the ladder to the wheelhouse and before he could get all the way up I kicked him in the chops and down he went. I got underway and things seemed to be under control. Everything is fine and as I was under the bridge something made me to look around and here came another guy up the ladder. This time I shut off the engines and hit that sob before he could think. Then I made a speech and guess they listened because I had no more trouble.

The engines started right up and I headed for the ship. As they were unloading the last guy that I hit waved at me and gave me a big smile.

I had that ship's crew on board several more times but with no more trouble.

I am going along out to one of the ships with a cargo of stores and no passengers. The boat I am running is one if the old slow boats and I am catching up with one of our fast boats so something is wrong. That boat might have engine trouble but as I am getting closer I can see the skipper on the after deck and it looks as though he is to be thrown over the side. I came up real close and told him to jump on board my vessel. Sure glad that he did without any argument. I jumped on board his boat and those guys cleared the deck and headed for the seating area.

I called the other boat and transferred him over to the chit-chat channel and told him the name and position of the ship to take the stores over to and make sure that you have the mate sign for them.

I know the name and position of the ship so went over there without any trouble.

I kind of like this water taxi job.

The boss called me into the office and looked very serious. "You must know that high-jacking a vessel on the high seas is a serious offence."

"What the hell are you talking about, I gave that guy my boat."

We had a good laugh and he shook my hand and told me that he is buying next time at the bar.

I came alongside that ship a few nights later and the only people that came on board my vessel were the Captain and his wife. Nothing was said about the other night until his wife asked me if I ran this boat all the time.

The Captain said, "Thanks for the other day and stopping what could have been very serious. I am sure that there will be no more trouble from this ship."

"Just part of the job but it would be nice if the word could get out to all the ships." I replied.

That ship weighed anchor and went to Sacramento for a load of grain.

I got my orders at the office and I am to go to pier 11 and pick up a pilot. He will tell you which ship and where to find it. That ship is in bound and I should get on board as close to the bridge as possible.

Here she comes, yep another Norwegian. Hope that they are better behaved.

After the ship had slowed down I came alongside and the bay pilot climbed up the ladder and the bar pilot came on down and boarded my boat.

The bar pilot is an old buddy and we got to visiting." What the hell did you do to that other ship a couple weeks ago? The scuttlebutt is that you beat up the crew and made them behave!"

"Aw, come on Bill, all I did was to make a few rowdies tow the mark."

"Well the word is out that you run a tight ship and will not let the crews act up."

"I expect the crews to have a good time but they had better run a straight course and pay attention to orders. And Bill, they can have three sheets to the wind but they had better not rattle my chain."

"Well I sure agree with that Capt."

There was no more trouble with that ship.

As I was going back to the ship on the second night after the trouble one of the women poked her head up from the seating area and asked to come up to the wheelhouse. "No stay below and don't bother me." She is a good looker and real tempting but orders are orders even for me!

That ship got underway and left the anchorage so now I won't have them to take care of. I am on the way to another ship and the radio started up and told me to come to the office and bring my logbook for the last 2 weeks.

I am at the office now and am wondering 'what now'.

The boss came in and asked me to go into his office. "That Greek ship that was in anchorage nine claims that you were late in getting the relieved crew off for their time in town."

"Well let's check my log book and since I write down all the times of arrival and departure we should be able to settle that problem."

I went over all the times for that ship and at last there it is. My arrival and departure times were a good half hour within the rules. They had no union but I guess someone on the beach had told them how we operate on our ships and so they figured that they could get in on some extra money. When we go to one of our ships and are late the whole crew gets overtime and that can be real expensive for the ship.

The boss asked to keep the logbook for a few days to show to the company attorney. " Sure, but get it back to me as soon as you can, and make sure that no one writes on the book."

" Anything else that we need to go over?"

" Nope, not that I can think of but now I am hungry and am going over to the Greek restaurant."

This time the boss said " Ok let's go get some of that good food."

We ordered and sat back with a glass of Greek wine and the first thing that he said was.

" Something is wrong with that Greek ship and their timekeeper."

I did not say anything but when the meal came the waiter said "Sorry about the problem with the ship."

Guess the info must be all over the waterfront and usually things like that get exaggerated and before long becomes a real big thing. I told him not to worry about it.

Nothing further was said about it and I guess that it is taken care of.

I am back on the boat doing some checking and making sure all is secure and in good shape. The radio barked again and I was told to come on up to the office. So here I go again.

"Sit down Capt and here is a cup of coffee."

Every time that he is so nice and even gets me a coffee I start to wonder. He shuffled papers on his desk, got up, sat down, and now I know that he has something big on his mind.

" Guess that you must have heard that we are thinking about having tours to Alcatraz Island?"

" Yes, I have heard a lot of talk about it. It seems to me that it would be a money maker."

" Sure do like your attitude. We will have a lot of officials from the city and the Park Service that want to see what is over there, and whether a boat can be put into the old prison dock."

"I can put the King into the old dock but nothing bigger. How many people or do you know for sure?"

" It looks like there will be about 40 all together. Even the Mayor is coming."

"You know that I don't have a regular crew and will need 3 deckhands and someone on the concession. I could do with 2 deckhands but the union says 3. I would appreciate at least 2 men that are experienced. The bar should be opened also as well as having coffee etc."

"It seems that you have it all figured out so be ready in two days. The passengers will be loading at 1000 hours and at Pier 41. They are to stay on the island as long as they want."

" Ok, will do."

" Thanks and I'm buying."

So off to the Eagle we go.

The whole deal worked out real well. The inspection of the island was a big success and they all want to start the tours as soon as possible.

The engineering dept. has to look at the landing on the island and make a ramp that can be used by any of the big boats. I offered to bring one of the big boats over to the island and meet with the engineers and show them what would be needed. They came over with me and were right on the ball. They got it all figured out and started the improvements.

I had to get back to the water taxis and worked for almost a month before they had everything in order for the tourists.

There are 2 English, 1 Norwegian, 1 Japanese, and 1 Danish ship in anchorage 9 that had to be taken care of.

We are contracted for 1 English, the Norwegian and the Danish ship. It will be necessary to bring to those ships, water, fuel, groceries as well as hauling crews back and forth.

I have on this trip men from each ship and they are OK from the ship to the dock. On the last crew trip from the dock to the ship the shit-hit-fan. It is about 0230 and the bars had closed a while ago and most of the men are drunk. It takes about 30 min. to run out to the first ship. The Danish ship was first in line so I went to it.

" Hey this is not my ship. What the hell is the matter with the Capt. He must be lost so I'll go up there and put him straight".

Well unless a man is invited up to the wheelhouse it is not a good place to just walk into.

He started to tell me that I should have gone to his ship first. That is as far as he got with his big mouth. " Get your ass out of my wheelhouse and get below before you get hurt". It worked because he did and we got back to business.

I started unloading the men from the Danish ship and one of the Norwegians slugged one of the Danes and all I could do was to back away from the ship and get a little room so that they could talk it all over. The Dane held his own and soon had the slugger out cold. Back to the ship and finished unloading the Danes.

The Norwegians were next but I decided to go to the Jap ship instead. Everyone was real quiet and not a word was said. I think that the Japs were really embarrassed and glad to get back to their own ship.

The Norwegians were subdued and just wanted to get to their ship. So , another night on the Bay.

On the way back to the dock the radio came on and the office wanted me to take the water taxi in the morning over to the island and check out the work that had been done on the docks.

Chapter 33

They did a good job and the docks look good.

"Take a boat and try out the new landing and if you think that they will do the job we will get someone else to do the water taxi and you get set up to do the Alcatraz run. Let us know what you need.

We got the advertising done and the crew all set up as to their duties.

"Tony go over to the island with me to look around. Bring flashlights and I will bring some chow." I didn't tell anyone that I wanted to go under the prison and look at the tunnels and cells that are there. We looked everything over and am surprised to see the chains and the holes where at one time prisoners were kept during the Military time when it was used as a prison.

The docking facility for the big boats looks really good and should work out real well. It will be necessary to put up gates in some places to keep the people away from danger and also paths should be marked to keep people in line. There will be times when 400 or more will be on the island. It will be the State Parks job to keep track of all those people.

Tony and I went back to the office and are in a meeting with the boss etc. "What do you think about the set-up?"

"It sure looks like a go and should work out fine. Lets take a group of 100 or so and give it a try and see if there will be any problems."

The boss said "Ok get the Princess ready and we will load on Sat. morning and give it a try. Tony talk to the Park people and make arrangements with them."

I like the way the boss makes a decision.

This is Wednesday and Tony and I went to the Eagle to get things all laid out. Joan, the head park person was sitting over in the corner at one of the tables and enjoying the view out the window. I came over to her and asked her if she wants to go over to the island. "When are we going?" was her ready reply. I told her. "Get your people ready and we are going to take 100 or so over on Saturday. If all goes well, the tours will start and it will be a regular run."

She knows Herb and Jim and also the concession girl and is happy they will be the crew. Now we have to talk this over so I got a round of drinks and before long we were making lots of trips with full loads.

Saturday is here and there are a lot of people on the dock waiting to load. After we got the count we had 220 on board. First day and a nice group.

Joan had gotten 6 park people to be on the boat and then go onto the island and guide the people around. Most people are really attentive and want to hear the history etc. about the island but it seems that some have to start moving away from the group to look on their own.

There are a lot of hazards on the island and people can get hurt. The park people are going to have those places blocked off and soon. The next trip over a group of workmen is on board.

We now have another job for the boats and the park people.

Very soon it has become apparent that the loading facility at pier 41 is not the right place. With all the people that are loading and getting off, some of the people are getting onto the wrong boats and instead of going to the island they are going on a regular bay tour and they get very unhappy.

It looks to me that Pier 411/2 would be a good place. The boss and I went over there and got it all figured out and set up. We had to put in a ticket booth and paths to follow. One for loading and one for off loading.

"Is this the ferry boat that goes to Tiburon?"

"No we are loading for Alcatraz." I told the young lady.

She said, " Well put up a sign so we won't get lost."

She has a good point, so now we have to get a sign done. Hope we don't have to teach people how to read.

We got the sign up and the ramps all fixed up and at last maybe we can just run the tour over to the island without problems.

The count on this load is 351 people. They are all excited and the park people will have their hands full.

Right off the bat people on the island started to sneak back into the line for the next tour, so now we have to get some more fencing done. Herding dumb cattle is easy but smart people are a real challenge. At times there will be 700 on the island. Last night the fencing was completed and we are ready.

It is a good thing that we have moved over to pier 411/2. There is a sea of people all the way to the street. Each person has to show his ticket in order to be allowed on board. One guy held out his hand and instead of a ticket he had a $100 bill and wanted to get aboard. Herb hollered up to me that he was trying to bribe him so I said" throw the cheat off the boat." He did and the people that were close enough to know what had happened gave him a big well done. The next day that same guy was in the line and bought a ticket. Tickets were being sold for $3.50 for an adult.

Another guy was in the line the next day and bought 10 tickets with the explanation that he had a group to go on board. We watched him and he turned out to be another cheat and was trying to sell those tickets for $10 each.

I have a day off and am wandering around the waterfront taking in the sights when a guy comes up to me and says "Hi Cap, where are you headed?"

"Just out watching people and later I am going to Frank's restaurant for supper."

" I will join you and buy if it is OK with you."

We got over to Frank's and sat down to order. I ordered steak and a bottle of wine. Don't get someone to buy every day. I am interested in what this guy is after because I have no idea who he is.

Sure enjoyed that meal and got up to leave and I asked him what his name is. He told me and said that he would see me tomorrow.

He was waiting on the dock when I got there. "Come on aboard and have a cup."

He told me a big story about how his Uncle had been a prisoner and had died on the island and sure would like the chance to go over there and stay for a while and see where he had been. (So now I know}

He wants a free shot at being on the island without going to the trouble of waiting in line and getting a ticket like every other person. I told him that he would have to get a ticket and it is still first come first served. He got upset and I got pissed and off the boat he went.

Chapter 34

The next day I was on Pier 41 and stopped to say hello to a couple buddies.

The ferry boat was just landing so I stopped to watch. There were only a few people to off load but one was being escorted off by one of the crew. I asked what the problem was and he told me that he is drunk as a skunk.

It seems that fellow had gotten onto the wrong boat and ended up at Tiburon. He was going to go to Alcatraz but he got lost. Anyhow he ended up over at Tiburon and since there were no more boats coming back to the City for 2 hours he went into the beer joint and the rest is history. The sad part is that now he is saying that it is the boats fault that he got drunk. The deckhand found out his address and called a cab and got the guy on his way home. Two days later he was in the line to buy a ticket so I went to him and asked him to come with me. I took him onto the boat and bought him coffee and told him to come up to the wheelhouse and ride with me.

It turned out that he had seen an attorney and was going to sue the company for getting him drunk etc. He changed his mind after riding with me and everything was healed over. This is sure an interesting job.

I just found out that the guy who wanted the free ride is a free lance writer and wanted a story. Too bad that he did not tell me that to begin with as I might have given him a chance.

We have fun on this job especially when we have a bunch of children on board. They are interested in everything and ask lots of questions. Herb and Jim know lots of facts and stories and enjoy having them for an audience.

We don't have a regular narration on the boat but on the island the Rangers and Park people do. They tell about what used to happen at the prison. Sometimes they even put people into a cell so that they can get a feel as to what it feels like to be locked up. There are times when a person will really get excited and start yelling and they will grab the bars and try to open them. They have to be let right out and then the ranger will have to get them over their fright and make sure that they will be OK. People are sure an interesting study.

Joan is up on the wing of the bridge during the loading of passengers. There were some boys, ages 12 or 14 that were pinching and poking the girls in the line. She turned to me and said "looks like I have some candidates for the cells today."

In each group of kids it seems like there is always one of them that has to be the big wheel. Joan told me later that that one became absolutely bonkers and made a big fool out of himself in front of the others. He was a little angel the rest of the trip. The cell treatment probably made a man out of the little brat.

I am on the last trip for the day and we are loaded and ready to head back to SF. Joan is in the wheelhouse with me, watching the people and relaxing and I asked her how the day went. She said that things were OK after the cell treatment.

I got Jim to take the wheel and I went on down to the main deck. Sitting in the corner were all those boys. They were real quiet and looked as though they had been through a real experience.

Joan had told me that when they were in the cell and she had left and turned the corner and was out of sight the boys came unglued. She left them by themselves for about 5 minutes and they were very scared

, hollering and banging on the bars. At last she let them out and they were little angels after that. Damned good lesson for them.

We docked and got the ramp up etc. and started to unload and as the boys were up on the dock the big bully looked up at me and said thanks for the trip.

This Alkatraz tour is actually getting more popular. It is raining hard and the line is long. We loaded 328 people on this trip and Paula is sure busy. The coffee sales are way up and she said "maybe we should be selling soup also."

The wind has not come up as it usually does when it rains. The visibility is sure lousy and I have to run on radar.

I called vessel traffic center and they advised me that there are two ships coming into the bay. One of them is entering the shipping lane and the other is in the deepwater lane. I am only interested in the one that is in the shipping lane as I will have to cross that lane so I called the ship. My old buddy Jack is the pilot and I told him that I would take his stern. He answered with a thank you. I really had the right of way but I sure am not going to argue with a ship.

The target on the radar showed me that he was almost abeam of the dock so I did not even try to leave until he was well past my position. That whole thing has taken about 5 minutes. Some guys I know would not wait and would get out there in the lane and out run the ship and put everyone in danger.

The other ship is almost in position so that maybe I can let her pass just ahead of me and maybe the people will be able to see her. She is a large container ship and is heading for Oakland. That worked out real well and the people got a good look. I had called that ship and told her what I was going to do.

Got over to the island and the landing was going to be rough. It is a fast running ebb tide and has caused the float and dock to jump around. I went on out away from there and waited for a little while and maybe it will settle down. Herb and Jim had their hands full keeping people back and out of the way. It did seem a little better after about 10 minutes so I came in to land again. I made it this time and we got tied up and off loaded in good shape. Several of the people told me how exiting it was and some even tried to give the deckhands tips. Never could figure out why people think that they have to be the first off because they have to wait for the park rangers after they get on the dock.

One day while they were waiting for the boat a helicopter swooped in and picked up two people that were in a hurry. They had called the office and had them call for the pick up. They had come from New York just for the tour and were running late and did not want to miss their return flight. Must have cost them plenty for that little caper.

Another time a speedboat landed at the old dock and four people hurried down there and got on. They took off in a big hurry and headed up toward the north. Must have been late for something.

We have been real busy and there has not been any time to really check over all the equipment etc. so I told the men to show up 2 hours early in the morning and we could do a better check.

Jim said," I can sure use some extra money as my daughter is still in college."

Herb also could use some extra money.

"Ok see you early then and thanks."

I made out the log and time sheet and turned them in to the office. The boss was at the boat before I got there in the morning.

"How come did you start early and are you thinking to do it again?"

"I needed more time in order to keep this boat in shape."

"We have people already on the payroll to do that"

I told him," Ok get them here to take care of it."

" Give me a list of the things that need taken care of."

"Ok I will make out a list as soon as I can."

It took me three days to get that list ready. It ended up 3 pages, both sides, and was a lot of detail. We'll see now what the boss thinks of that.

I was on my 2nd trip and the radio started transmitting and it was the boss. He told me to come to the office as soon as we were tied up this evening.

On the way to the office I ran into a couple of my fellow skippers and they said "Oh, Oh we heard the boss telling you to come to the office. We wish you the best of luck."

Sure made me feel great! Oh well, I can always go back to the tugs.

I rapped on the boss's door and he said, " Come on in and sit down."

He sat there in his chair and did not say anything for a good couple minutes and then only, "Explain".

" Ok, I gave you a list of things that need to be done on my boat. All the boats need the same, to be looked at more closely."

He said," How in the hell can all those things be done?"

"Please be at my boat in the morning and I will show you what I am talking about."

" Oh balls, let's go to the Eagle."

"Only if you promise to be at my boat in the morning."

He promised and gave me a big smile.

We walked over to the Eagle and when we got up to the bar I told Danny that I am buying.

His reply was," what's the occasion?"

I told him that this may be my last chance cause I'm on the list again.

Of course Danny replied," I am going to stay out of this one for sure."

" Oh bull shit, don't believe a word of it," said the boss.

Anyhow we got things settled pretty well that night.

I'm at the boat waiting for the boss and here he comes. First things first and that is to get a cup of coffee.

Now it is time to get down to business.

Ok let's go and check the engine room. I put the key into the engine room door and as usual it would not turn. Got the lock open finally and we went down to the engine room. As I went by the top of the ladder the top bolt is still loose and the rail going down wobbles but I don't think that the boss noticed. I checked the engines, oil, water, the generators, pumps, shaft etc. were ok.

I started up the engines and checked the pressures and pointed to the ladder and waved to go up. Too noisy down there to talk.

"You got the engines started and checked over and now what do you need extra time for?" asked the boss.

" Yes the engines are going and you probably think that is all we need to do to get underway. Look at the list that I had given to you and you will see that I only checked about 15 items. There are another 35 to 40 items that I have not had time to check. Please realize that all the boats need a real check over once in awhile. It is not necessary to come in early each day." Was my reply.

There are already at least 300 people waiting for the boat to load and we have to keep on a schedule.

"Capt. Come to the office when you are done for the day."

We have had a good run for the day with full loads each trip. Now it is up to the office.

First thing that the boss said was," I have been on this time thing all day and have come to this decision. You are to do what you need to as far as coming in early but when you do I want you to make out a special log sheet so we will know what is going on."

" Does that mean the this time thing will be left up to me?" I asked just to make sure.

"Sure thing. Use your own judgment."

"Ok, now that that is settled I'm headed for the Eagle."

" You mean that after all that you are not going to invite me?" asked the boss.

" Yeah, ok let's both go."

" Now that I'm also a time keeper as well as doing my regular job I'll give you the honor of buying a drink." I told him.

The boss is quick and said " Let's play high card and the one with the high one gets to buy."

So I asked Danny for a deck and the boss shuffled and I cut. I got a king and he had a big smile and now he got a card and he got an ace. That started the evening. We went over to Chic's for supper and had a good time.

There is one more job that I do and don't mind it a bit. It seems as though I have been chosen to be "Uncle' to the park rangerettes.

"Hello Linda how're you doing?"

"Ok Capt., but can I ride with you?"

"Sure can." She is one real cute gal about 25 years old. So I gave her a big hug and cleared off a seat for her. It seems to be boyfriend trouble again.

I let her talk about him coming home late chewing tobacco, getting drunk and in general being a big ass-hole, as far as she is concerned.

"What the hell, are you so goodie that he thinks that he has to [show you] ?" is the first thing that I am telling her. She looks surprised. I suppose she thinks that I should be nice.

"Do you cook, clean and treat him like he is a man?" I asked.

"Oh I do and I like sex but he treats me as though I am not even there."

"Well I'll bet you that you tell him that he is not going fast enough or aren't you done yet? Or maybe you say that you are not interested now.

She did not answer me and I believe that I have hit a sore spot. She just looked at me and big old tears came into her eyes.

We are coming in to the island and she said that, " I am going to get off and talk to Angie. She is just finishing up with that group. Thanks for the talk and it sure gives me something to think about."

I bet that she will be back for another session later.

Got tied up and we are almost ready to unload

We have 350 on board this trip.

The vessel traffic center made a general broadcast that there is a ship just at the north end of the island and was headed for Oakland. I grabbed the PA mike and told the crew to hold up the unloading and to clear the float and get the door shut. The weather is perfect and no wind and we should have a good safe day but not with that ship coming. The ship is in the deep water channel and will be coming real close to the island. If it is going over 6 knots it will make a big wake that could make it hazardous for us real quick.

The crew acted real well and got the orders followed and even yet they had no idea what was taking place. I went back on the mike and told them about the ship and to get all the people possible to sit down and at least hold on.

By the time that the wake hit there was only one person left on the ramp and he held on.

The boat made contact with the dock and rode up onto the bottom of the rub rail. I was able to get the boat back away from the dock but we left some paint there.

"Vessel Traffic center. Tell that ship off Alkatraz to slow down as it caused me trouble at the passenger float. He made a big wake and we are lucky not to have any injuries that I know of as yet. If we have I will call you back."

I am fortunate to have a good experienced crew or we could have had injuries. They acted without any hesitation and got things secured right away. I guess that pilot will get into trouble. Sure hope that I don't get called in for a hearing. I probably know the pilot.

Got all the people loaded and headed back to SF.

The radio came alive and it was not on the official channel but on our BS channel. My buddy told me that the dock is full of reporters and cops. Looks like we have gotten famous again.

I came close and made the turn for the dock and what I saw sure was not pretty. I called the office and told them to clear the dock and get those people back and out of the way. We have to unload and can not do so with all the commotion there. The boss told me to stand off and he will call when it is safe to land.

The newspapers must be tuned in to the vessel traffic center channel. I see that there are several lawyers on the dock as well. Sure are a bunch of leeches. The people that are on the boat were not on board when the big wake hit us but maybe they will tell a lot of { what if's and yeah buts} and we know that the newspapers love that. My men won't even tell them the time of day.

The dock is finally cleared so now I can land and unload.

The reporters and the lawyers swarmed onto the passengers as soon as they had gotten up the dock. Reminds me of a bunch of hogs going after the feed as soon as it is poured out into the trough.

Paula had to go up the dock and get some things for the snack bar and is having a hard time getting through the crowd. She is almost being stopped. I got onto the PA system and turned it up to high and told those people to let her pass and leave her alone or I will call the cops. That stopped them and she went about her business.

I have to be careful and not let any of those pests on the boat for the next trip. I told the crew to watch for them.

The people at the ticket booth have quit selling tickets. Good thing too as some of those reporters have tried to buy tickets for the return run. Sure be glad when this day is over.

At last we have the boat loaded and we can get on our way. Herb told me later that he had been offered $100 by one of them to get onto the boat. I backed out and made my turn and headed for the island. There is a small boat running along with us and it looks like trouble. I called the island and told them to lock the gate at the small boat dock.

I came on in and made fast at the dock and started unloading. Sure am glad that the gate at the small boat dock is secured. There are four people there, shaking there fists at me so I gave them the finger. Ha ha fixed them up good.

The people that are loading were on the boat when the big wake caused the trouble.

We got loaded and headed for the city. I got on the PA and made a speech about what they can expect at the dock when we unload. One of them said to me" how about unloading at the other dock, it is only one block from the usual place." Man, that guy has a good idea. I called the office and asked the boss if I could come into there as my starboard rudder is fowled. He said "sure but let's not make a habit of this".

He is standing on the dock as I am making my landing and could see right off that both of the rudders are working well.

I explained to the passengers that it was necessary to unload here in order to be clear of all the reporters and lawyers. "Anyone that has trouble walking the extra block let me know and I will get you a cab." No one complained and the remarks that I heard thought that I was right in making the diversion. After they were all off I went back over to the other dock and all those pests were sure pissed off. Got to have some fun.

The cops were at the dock and one of them came on the boat and met with me. He was real happy that I had out-foxed those reporters etc. They had been expecting a big problem.

Now I have to go back to the Island and pick up all the people that are there.

Joan came up to the wheelhouse and was happy that this day is over. She told me that the small boat that had been trying to unload left and headed towards SF. She asked to use the PA system. She told the passengers that the dock should be clear by now and that they would have no more trouble.

I don't see any reporters on the dock so I came on in and got the people unloaded. We were cleaning up and getting ready to secure the boat when two men walked right on and asked, "Are you the captain of this boat?"

"Sure am and you were not invited to come on board so get off."

They started to give me some lip so I keyed the radio and told the office to send a cop to this boat now. Those two guys ran off in a hurry. I had the night button secured on the radio so no transmission had gone through. Got rid of them quick.

Chapter 35

It is almost that time again when we have to bid for runs and I am thinking about putting in for the oil recovery boat. She is not a conventional boat and is built only for oil work and is a challenge to run.

My buddy Ed had run that boat about a year or so ago and I will have him tell me about how to run her. "I'll meet you at the Eagle after we get done for the day."

We have been here at the Eagle for about an hour and I am hungry. "Let's go to Greeks for supper."

He replied, "Sure thing and you can buy. After all you are learning all about running that boat."

He sure got me on that one so off to the Greeks we go.

We had walked down a ways when I made the remark that those sea gulls are sure up late. Ed said, "sea gulls hell, that is someone hollering for help."

All the skippers have keys for the docks so we opened the gate and went down to the float. Sure was someone there. Poor guy was in the water and since the float is about 4ft. high and impossible to reach the deck from the water he was going to drown. " Let's lay down on the float Ed and maybe we can get a grip on the poor guy."

We reached down as far as possible and the guy raised one arm and I got a hold of his wrist and Ed got a hold on his other arm and we heaved up and were able to get him up onto the deck. He was not very big and a good thing too as it was all we could do to raise him.

Ed started first aid and I went up to the street to get aid. A cab was approaching so I stopped it and the driver got on his radio and called for an ambulance. It came within 5 minutes and got that guy on the way to the hospital real quick.

The Greek's was only a little ways further and we got washed up and sat down for supper. The Greek hovered around and was hoping for a run down on what happened and we finally told him.

He listened to every word and at last said," hold it right there and I am going to tell you about 3 guys that had been in here about 1 hour ago. They were talking about some thing that must have just happened and that their ride should be here in a minute. One of them mentioned that some guys can swim for a long time but that water is sure cold."

The Greek went over to wait on a man that sat over at the bar and when he came back to us he continued. " It was only about 5 minutes later that the door opened and a guy waved at those guys and they jumped right up and headed out. One of them had put a $5 bill onto the table for the coffee. Pretty good tip for sure."

I asked " did you notice anything about how they were dressed and how big were they?"

" They had on working clothes, like long shoremen but were clean. Each were big men. The guy at the door wore a suit, but no tie. I could hear the car take off in a big roar and fast."

Ed and I just sat there and knew that the men were the one's that had put the man into the water.

I said " guess we had better get to the hospital and talk to him."

"Don't say anything to anyone about this as it looks bad and remember that you could get hurt if they hear what you have just told us."

We got a cab and went to the emergency hospital and it dawned us that we don't know his name. Now what to do? Right then the door to the emergency room opened and the guy on the gurney is the man we need to talk to. So we followed and found his room. There is no one around so we just went right into the room and had to wait for a few minutes and he stirred and at least is awake. He opened his eyes and spotted us.

He knew who we were right off and said that he is sure glad to see us. " After I tell you what happened watch yourselves and be careful!"

He looked at the door and I went and looked out and no one was around so he continued. " This is a union beef and three guys had been sent to kill me and make it look like an accidental fall. Well you guys came along at the right time or they would have succeeded. The union will be billed for this treatment and that is bad because I am still alive."

I said," Bill I am going to the office and I will be right back."

"Ok Henry we'll be here." He answered.

It is lucky that I had just got some money the day before so up to the office I went.

Sitting at the desk is a real pretty thing and turned out to be easy to talk to. All of a sudden I realized that I did not know our friends name but he is the only one in room 6. "When will the man in 6 be able to leave? The nurse said that he should be able to go home now."

"Well I will check." She said and crossed those legs again.

She made a call up to floor where he is and in about that much time she said " the nurse feels as though he can go anytime."

"How much is the bill?"

She said that the union will be billed.

" I want to pay his bill right now, please."

Guess that is the right thing to say because she answered, "Great, that will save paper work. Let's see room, emergency etc. hmm, paying cash. The whole bill is, are you ready for this? "

I'm standing there with my fingers crossed and she came up with," That will be all together $298."

It so happened that I had 3 one hundred dollar bills in my pocket, which I had been saving, so there they go.

She asked my name and I told her Henry so that is what she put on the receipt.

I said," Lady, keep the change and thanks."

Back to the room I told them to get ready and let's go as soon as possible.

We got outside and there is a cab right in front so in we go.

All of a sudden our passenger said," let me out here and thanks for everything."

"What is that guy's name." I asked Ed.

He answered with," Hell I don't know."

"We have to get to work. Take us to Pier 41 driver."

That is one more episode in our life on the waterfront in SF.

I got to the boat and had only about 10 minutes to get ready to sail. I got the engines started and the passengers were almost all loaded by that time.

We got underway and Herb brought me a cup of coffee. He hung around and hemmed and hawed and I knew he wanted an explanation so all I said was, "that sure was something."

He finally gave up and after awhile here came Jim and after that Paula came up but no one got any other answer. Had to be quiet about things.

It all was forgotten later so back to the routine. I have to make up my mind about the oil recovery boat as that bid is coming up soon. That boat has only the skipper and one other man. The man comes out of the union and some are not good to sail with. No more having a steady crew.

Chapter 36

I decided to bid that run anyhow and sure enough I got the bid. All the men have to come from the union hall and they are all told the special things that they will have to do and wear before they are dispatched. Well some of them are so thick headed that they might as well have talked to the bulkhead.

They are not allowed to work on the Spill Spoiler if they do not have on cotton, wool or natural material clothes. There is always a threat of fire around oil and gasoline. Polyester, nylon or that kind of clothes can just melt around the body and the wearer would not have a chance. Any shoes that have nails can make a spark on the metal decks and are not allowed.

I am surprised how many men just don't get those few directions and end up having to go back to the union.

I checked the boat over and found out that it is very low on fuel, first thing is to fuel up.

There is a guy up on the dock just standing and looking around. "What do you want?", I hollered.

He said that he was assigned this boat. He had a dinner bucket in his hand and was smoking a cigar. Dam, another guy that is sure not a sailor.

"Put out that cigar and come aboard. There is no boat up there on the dock". He threw the cigar into the drink and came aboard. Most sailors would put out the cigar and the bitter end would end up in his pocket for future use. This guy had thrown away almost a whole cigar.

He got aboard and then I noticed that he had on nylon and polyester clothes. "Let me see the bottoms of your shoes." I asked.

His reply," One at a time or both at once."

"Get your ass off this boat and go back to your union. You were told the rules about dress."

I got on the radio to the office and ordered another sailor. About an hour later another came and I know this man. We had sailed together at one time in the past. He had on the right clothes and now I can get to work. Got him signed aboard and finished up the paper work.

"Let's go get fuel." I started the engines and Jack sure knew about casting off lines etc.

There are no tankers out in the bay at this time so after fueling I went out where there is room and just played around learning how to run this crazy boat.

I went back to the dock and just got tied up and the radio is coming alive. Vessel Traffic center is talking to a tanker that is under the bridge and in bound. She is to go to anchorage #9 and anchor for a few days. Looks like we are to be busy. Sure glad to have a sailor aboard.

While I was out practicing running this boat Jack had been learning about the oil recovery equipment.

The wheelhouse on this boat is about 15 feet up a vertical ladder and takes two hands to climb. Jack hollered up and asked "do you want your coffee served up there or do you want to come down?"

I came on down and he not only had coffee ready he had also made a sandwich. Like I said, he is a good sailor.

Went back up after eating and I started with a full cup of coffee up the ladder. Most was still in the cup when I got to the wheelhouse but was a wonder. I had better bring a thermos on board next trip.

The radio came alive and the pilot on the tanker told me to be at #9. I know the pilot so he was easy to talk to. Trying to get things done by talking to a foreign crewmember is sometimes impossible. He had it all organized so when we came astern the tanker there were men to take our line and make fast.

We held astern the tanker real well and if there were a leak , any oil would show up at our boat. Our job is to stay alert and ready for action. We were relieved 10 hours later. We went back to the dock in a water taxi.

Next day we went back out but instead of going to the same ship we went to another. This one is loaded with hi grade Arabian Light and can be very dangerous. The fumes are really powerful and it is a good thing that most of them are blown away. There is an air indicator on board and it is reading almost in the red. No way could Jack heat coffee or anything so I am glad that I have my thermos. This will be a long day.

The wind has picked up and it is causing the boat to hold off at an angle and is necessary to keep the engine running in order to keep from going around and against the tanker. Now most of the fumes are blown away so the breathing is better. We had these conditions for another 5 hours and then the boat came on around where it is supposed to be so I shut down the engines. Here comes the water taxi and our relief.

I told the relief skipper about the having to run the engines and he said, "yeah, yeah I will run this boat now."

"Come on Jack let's go and did you bring the thermos."

"No, but I will get it."

He got over to the scupper and opened the thermos and made like he was pouring the rest of the coffee out. It was empty but he made a point.

I am in the ready room reading a story and enjoying the day when the radio made a report that there is a tanker coming in from sea. Guess we will have another job.

The tanker that is loaded with the Arabian Light is on her way to Chevron to be unloaded. Maybe the one coming in will have crude oil aboard.

Jack came in and said that he was in the office and they told him that we are to be at the tanker by 1500 hours.

"Ok, I will get up to the office and get the papers. I would send you but I have to sign them. I will make sure to say hello to the secretary."

Jack looked at me with that long face so I said

"Come on with me and you can say hello again." He brightened up real quick. I know why he spends so much time in the office.

The last entry in the logbook for fueling was over a week ago so we had better check the fuel. We have time to top off.

We topped off and headed out to the tanker. This one is loaded with crude and the wind is down and everything looks great.

This tanker is to unload in 2hrs and we will be turned loose soon.

The radio came on and told me to go to #5 as soon as you can. The water taxi came to the tanker and put a pilot aboard. He told me that they will let go the tie up line in a few minutes.

We got underway for #5 and here comes the Sheriff Patrol boat. I came dead in the water and he came alongside. " You are to go directly to #5 and make sure that you have no contact by radio with anyone. I will escort you."

I have no idea what is going on but I will follow the orders.

"Hurry up, we have to be there."

I signaled him that I have this boat full ahead and we can go no faster.

We finally got to the tanker and got tied up astern. Coast Guard, safety, drug and several other agencies were put aboard the tanker.

Two important looking men were put on my boat and we were not allowed to talk to them. I guess that they are to be aboard in case a bad guy tries to leave the tanker.

Jack and I did our job and watched for an oil leak. Nothing happened and we were relieved 5 hours later.

A man jumped off the tanker and was not able to swim against the currant and ended up at our boat. Those two men got him on board and handcuffed him and put him onto the Sheriff's boat. When we relieved that crew there were two new men on board but this time they had FBI badges on.

The good thing about all this is that hot coffee and food is brought and a whole lot more than those men could eat so Jack and I did real well.

That tanker had been moved out to #9 so we went out there to relieve that crew. Things are back to normal. Never was able to find out what the trouble was.

She was moved after about 5 hours and since there are no other tankers around we went on in to the dock.

Good time to check everything and decided to top off the fuel. We got her full and everything else is in good shape.

It is about noon and all of a sudden the emergency sounded and we were told to get underway. There is a spill up by Richmond clear up to the Richmond Bridge. Now we will earn our keep. Sure glad that we had checked the boat and were ready.

Chapter 37

I lit off the engines and Jack singled up the lines and off we go. I blew the siren and made a big show for the tourists. One boat was coming in and he made a quick turn and got out of the way so I put the engines full ahead and off to war we go. Oil spills are no fun and this one is a big one I'm to find out.

The tide is on the end of the flood and so we should be able to get on the spill at the beginning of the ebb.

We are just abeam of Richmond and ahead I can see the tell-tale brown discoloring of the spill. Looks to me that the oil must be crude oil. Jack was right on the ball and got the gear ready. Traffic center had already alerted ships etc. so I did not have them in the way.

Slowed down and Jack lowered the belts into the water and started them turning. It is exactly 1hour since we got the warning about the spill. Pretty darn good time. I can see the tug and barge coming that will load the oil that we pick up. We only hold 500gallons and we will need to pump out many times. Crude oil will start to solidify after about 30 hours in the cold water so we have to work fast.

The barge comes alongside when I call for it and if we are in the right spot we can keep the belts running while Jack pumps out. This is not in the "book" but is working out for us.

I lost track of the number of times we pumped out. Good thing that the barge is big. We worked all night, the next day and the next night. No stopping and both Jack and I are getting tired.

The oil finally got so stiff that we were not able to do much with it. Another operation started and we were secured.

This new bunch would get the oil surrounded with floats and they would pick it up with rakes and shovels.

We went to the dock and got tied up. I had been in the wheelhouse for a straight 36 hours and am sure ready for time off. Jack was beat too and next thing is a shower and some food.

The showers are up the street about a block away and Jack and I have not even gotten up the ramp when we were approached by cameramen and reporters. Dam it to hell.

Jack and I turned around and went back aboard the boat. I got on the radio and talked to the office and told them that we have been invaded by those people and to call the cops.

Guess the boss figured that this is a good chance to get some publicity so here he comes down the dock. They are doing a lot of arm waving and talking. He hollered to me that " these people want to come aboard to check it out and is that OK with you?'

I replied " hell no, we have been on a bad spill and the decks are covered with oil and are slippery. You may come on down the ramp but stay off the boat."

They came down the ramp and the cameras are sure busy.

" What is your name Cap and is this man your only crew?"

Jack and I went into the crew quarters and shut the door behind us. So much for our showers. I want to hear what the boss is saying but don't want to get that close. They b-s'd out there for a good 30 minutes and then they took off.

Jack and I waited another 10 minutes and then we went up the ramp and checked to see if all is clear.

We got our showers and then headed for Chic's for some of his good food.

Not one word is said about the spill and we enjoyed the dinner. Afterwards we went into the bar and here comes Chic and he sat with us. The conversation got around to the spill so we filled him in on what happened.

He said," sure glad it is over."

Jack added," that the good thing about it all is the paycheck."

" See you later Chic, I'm going to hit the sack and sleep for a couple days."

Got to my camper and did get into the sack.

"Heah, are you going to sleep forever."

I rolled over and looked at the clock. I have slept for 16 hours. Wow.

"You have a tanker about 6 hours from now. She will be coming into the bay pretty soon."

"OK boss I will get moving." I had to get dressed and head for the boat but first I am going to get some chow. I went back to Chic's.

In walked Jack and he had the empty thermos with him.

This bid is over and now I am running the ferry and tour boats and have more or less steady hours again.

About the Author

He has run all the boats in the story. It is first hand information
and enjoyed all of it